Jesus Is Sending
You This Message

Also by Jim Grimsley

Algonquin Books
Winter Birds
My Drowning
Comfort & Joy
Mr. Universe and Other Plays
Boulevard

Meisha Merlin Publishing
Kirith Kirin

Scribner
Dream Boy

Tor Books
The Ordinary
The Last Green Tree

University of Texas Press
Forgiveness

Jesus Is Sending You This Message

[STORIES]

Jim Grimsley

With an Introduction
by Dorothy Allison

 alyson books
NEW YORK

The story titled "We Move on a Rigorous Line" is adapted from the title of a story by Samuel R. Delany ("We, in Some Strange Power's Employ, Move on a Rigorous Line").

Manufactured in the United States of America

A trade paperback original published by Alyson Books
245 West 17th Street, New York, NY 10011

Distribution in the United Kingdom by Turnaround Publisher Services Ltd.
Unit 3, Olympia Trading Estate, Coburg Road, Wood Green
London N22 6TZ England

First Edition: October 2008

08 09 10 11 12 13 14 15 16 17 a 10 9 8 7 6 5 4 3 2 1

ISBN-10: 1-59350-100-5
ISBN-13: 978-1-59350-100-6

Library of Congress Cataloging-in-Publication data are on file.

Cover design by Victor Mingovits
Interior design by Charles Annis

For Doris Betts

CONTENTS

INTRODUCTION

"Goddamnit."

I first met Jim Grimsley on the page—among the haunted, word-driven images of *Winter Birds*. I remember reading the manuscript sitting out back of our home with the redwood trees around me, and putting my head back as if I were back among the pines and scuppernong vines of my childhood home in South Carolina. The language and the images took me up and wrung me hard. That family was as familiar to me as my own, that restless desperation and overwhelming sense of danger all too real. The ache to run away and fall into the arms of the dangerous lover— River Man or Red Dirt Woman—so patently present, I felt as if I were again fourteen and digging my fingernails into my palms to keep from doing something sudden, or stupid, or painfully normal. "Who is this guy?" I whispered out loud. Then I went in to write the editor at Algonquin that I loved this book as if it were my own.

It was a year later that I met Jim in the real—at a public event at Charis Books in Atlanta, Georgia. He came up to me with a diffident smile and a hesitation I recognized immediately. Queer without doubt, raised poor in the South, good manners, and a sense of humor in bright squinty eyes—I knew immediately all those things. Then he said his name, and I wanted to climb over the table between us and put my arms around him. This was that guy. He looked so young to me, but I was tired and feeling old.

"Son," I said. "Damn it! You can write."

He laughed. It was a good laugh, open and easy—restrained only by the close throng of fierce young lesbian feminists who looked at him uncertainly. I had no uncertainty. Jim felt to me like a cousin, an escapee, someone like me, one who knew just how fragile people like us were in the world. He felt like family of the best kind, a writer who had saved himself in story, made sense of what made no sense, and created on the page a glory that fed his soul and mine.

Is there anything more powerful than the poetry wrung from hard-learned compassion?

Is there anything more stubborn than a child raised to hate the self, who, none the less, chooses love?

Choosing compassion and love, without compromising what is all too painfully known, is not what we generally speak about when we talk about literature—but it is what I treasure in the best writing. It is what I go to a story to find—understanding of the deepest kind and a shared sense of what is true. How, after all, do we know what is true in a world where so many lie so easily and persistently? It is not in the daily news that we find the reality of

"The Moral Imagination" ~ Robert Coles

our lives, but in the shared stories of not only what has happened or is happening, but what it all means. The story teller becomes the mediator, the lens through which all is focused and rendered sharper and more revelatory.

The revelations in the stories you will find here are sharp as razors and just as hard and strong as tusks. Yes, these are southern stories, gay stories, romances, and lyric realism that will show you a grace of insight made even more startling by the everyday, matter-of-fact people whom Jim Grimsley renders with compassion. You will find too those flashes of that wry, wonderful sense of humor I treasure. How does trash survive? We laugh a lot, sometimes ruefully, sometimes in appalled recognition, at what others find not humorous at all. And sometimes, we laugh to keep from crying. We are not much for crying—we were raised to take a deep breath and do what had to be done. Crying can get in the way of that, but laughing moves us forward. Sometimes in the world we inhabit, a short bark of a laugh is the only response that makes sense. Jim Grimsley can laugh with the best of us.

And Jim can sing.

Oh, yes, you will find song here—not that lovely tenor I have heard him use—but song, the use of language to sift and shift and polish experience.

One of the best memories of my life is a morning in Durham, North Carolina, when Jim stood alone on a stage and instead of reading a story, sang one—a gospel he had written. "I dreamed I saw my father walking by the sea . . ."

It was a conference on violence, but everything we had talked about for two days was remade when Jim lifted his chin and began to sing. Tears came to my eyes, and I could feel the whoosh of emotion and memory flood through me for what Jim sang echoed what I had loved and lost in the Baptist Church and what I had treasured and walked away from as an angry young lesbian treated with suspicion and resentment by my enormous working-class family.

Poetry.

Song.

Gospel.

Something of the soul persists even in a world that holds us in such unrelenting contempt and fear.

We are more than what we are said to be. We are larger and finer, and yes, absolutely vital to the community that does not know our worth. We, in our specific complicated astonishing stories, enlarge the possibility of all people.

Here are the dead, and the surviving. Here are the best and worst of us—and occasionally the mysterious scary among us. Here are the gorgeous, sexy, startling, and completely mesmerizing creations of the remarkable Jim Grimsley. Take a deep breath and get ready. You need what you are going to find here.

—Dorothy Allison, June 2008

Jesus Is Sending
You This Message

THE VIRTUAL MAIDEN

SHE had come to clean, thick-waisted, holding a dustpan, her lower lip slack. Moving methodically and ponderously across the wide apartment, she carefully swept the broad hardwood floors, scrubbed every square inch of countertop with cautious circular motions of the sponge, and used a soft, old toothbrush to remove each tiny thread of grime from the corners of the molding of all forty-eight cabinet doors in our kitchen. In the bathroom she scrubbed with one eco-friendly brand and deodorized with another, followed by a special organic antibacterial agent guaranteed to massacre germs in massive numbers, with Randall there to instruct her in what she should use and when. She pushed the vacuum cleaner across the carpet, employing such care near any object like a table leg or baseboard that it appeared at moments that her whole self was placed into the space between the rubber bumper on the old Electrolux and the object toward which it rolled.

Randall and I had outgrown our need for disaster. I no longer believed he would someday wash all the dishes he used between meals if I simply let them pile up in the sink. I no longer believed there was any place safe from his dirty socks—albeit of a fine cashmere blend—or his abandoned Calvin Klein boxer briefs. He was apt to drop his clothing in the oddest places, on the way to the kitchen or in the foyer behind the schefflera that he had picked out and I watered. I no longer believed he would have the grace to make the bed when he finally crept out of it at eleven in the morning, more than likely to answer the phone, which would be me calling, worried he would sleep till sundown.

So we hired a maid. Or, to be more specific, Randall hired her.

Randall has money, of course. He works nights as a bartender at that disco downtown with the long lavender neon and chrome bar stocked with every type of liquor ever distilled. I suppose nobody calls it a disco anymore, but that's what it is. Everybody goes to Spunky's. There's supposed to be a sex club in that neighborhood, a gay sex club, and sometimes when I'm visiting Randall at work, I try to imagine which of the young men are coming to Spunky's for a drink before heading to the club to do whatever they do over there. It's the young men, of course, not the older ones, that I imagine as being the perfect candidates for the kind of cheap physical encounter that used to bring me such bliss. Now I am as far from any of them as if I had come here on a boat from Asia and spoke not one word of their language. They change their slang for the same reason they change the addresses of the sex clubs constantly: so we older ones won't find out, won't show up with our unfortunate, tired bodies and sagging behinds. I have Randall, of course, but I keep him well, and he appreciates that, feels a genuine affection for me; and, besides, he has this job where he is a star among the other stars, at the bar that everyone goes to. Randall tells me about the sex clubs sometimes when he visits after his shift at the bar, but I hardly listen. He's still young and wanted in a place like that. But most of the time he gets enough attention at the bar at Spunky's that he's happy to come home after work. Randall has money, he makes good money at the bar, that's what got me started on this; Randall, in fact, has his money and mine, so I suppose he's actually the richer. It is a fact, after all, that he found Constance and hired her.

When she pronounces the name, the sound comes out nothing like the spelling. Her control over her tongue and her voice is far from consummate and the sound is more like, "Cuhon-san . . ." with the N-consonant sound at the end drifting outward and dying to nothing just at the edge of the S-consonant. She with her eyebrows run together and the heavy upper lids to her eyes that tell me she has come to clean and not to have a conversation. That tell me she is some sort of special-needs person. She glances furtively at me and ducks her head and shuffles to the cleaning closet with her lower lip hanging and her very moist pink tongue almost in sight.

I am sorry; I have lapsed into the present moment, as if she were here, right in front of me, but of course she isn't.

The first day I saw her, when Randall introduced me to her—Randall Cruz with his perfect face, like that picture on the cover of *The Persian Boy*, the Michelangelo drawing—Randall stood in my kitchen beside this lumpish mouse-eyed thing in a dress that was too tight across the middle, the fabric drawn taut across her navel, obscenely large. He introduced her and she ducked her head and looked up at me, her eyebrows like someone's fake mustache. "Please to know," she said, in the softest voice, and the "you" died away like the end of her name. She immediately stuck a nail in her teeth and worked her thumb there, and Randall took her wrist and gently pulled the hand away. So gently. Gazing at her with an expression on his face like nothing I'd ever seen there before.

"Come with me, sweetie," he said. "I'll show you where to start."

A few moments later she was on her hands and knees scrubbing the toilet in the guest bath; though I only glanced at her, I could feel the force of her concentration, her fierceness, as she guided the brush along the inside of the bowl, using the organic and unscented bathroom cleaner Randall insists on, though it's ludicrously expensive and we have to drive all the way across town to Rainbow Foods to find it.

She moved, heavy and methodical, from one end of the house to the other. When she was done, hours later, Randall pressed five twenty-dollar bills into the correct pocket of her billfold and handed it back to her. She gazed at the green bills in awe and moved her head to follow them when they disappeared into the wallet. She looked at the money again and again.

"Can I borrow your keys?" Randall asked. "I need to take her home. My car's in the shop."

I handed him the keys. I gave him the look that is supposed to communicate the telepathic message *You and I need to have a serious discussion.* He ignored this, as he does all my telepathic messages, sending them careening off his smooth forehead to splatter against the nearest wall. He said, "Come on, Connie, let's go home now," and she smiled and gazed at him with the same adoration as before. He walked with her at her very slow pace to the door.

When he had navigated Connie down the back steps of the deck, heading to the parking garage underneath the complex, I took a long inspection tour. Our bedroom spread out in the neat lamplight, the room tidy and pristine, not an undergarment in sight. The bathrooms, both-and-a-half of them, were immaculate, and I am tempted to say the brass faucets gleamed like new, though the truth is I never saw them new; the place was ten years old when I moved in.

I should tell you about the man who sold me the apartment, the man whose story was haunting me at the time that Connie first started to clean the place. The man's name was MacNeal Crook and he called himself Neal, of course, and wore silk ascots, actually wore them, perfectly tied and fluffed at the neck, and also wore one of those goatees that looked as though it had been drawn in black marker on his chin. His hair was peppered gray but his beard was black as a crow. I know he must have dyed it since a man's chin will nearly always gray before his head does. One had to look at him and wonder why he would color his beard and not his hair, but if he had colored his hair as black as his beard, he would have looked like a pair of patent leather shoes. He kept the apartment full of gardenias he bought at a local nursery. Some were beginning to brown the morning we met to talk about the condo. I had known Neal for a very long time, since he was in college, and he had been the fussy dresser even in those early days at Sewanee. But he had decided to move to Morocco now and wanted to sell his apartment, and I obliged him by buying it at over the appraised value. He had transferred to a job in Morocco with some oil company; at least, I believe it was an oil company, though if it was, maybe it was Saudi Arabia to which he was moving, or Kuwait. Though Morocco rings a bell. What made him special, memorable, aside from the unforgettable scent of rotting gardenia blossoms in his apartment, was his collection of pornography. I had always thought of him as a gay man, like me, naturally, but it turned out he had an extensive collection of films and photographs of prepubescent and just-postpubescent girls. One whole walk-in closet was full of the tapes and stacks of glossy prints. There was a separate filing cabinet for slides. He showed me some of them and I tasted nausea at the back of my throat as the slides popped onto the pale wall, pasty-fleshed young girls with sharp hip bones, swollen nipples that were budding into breasts, and smatterings of pubic hair. He couldn't take this collection with him to a Muslim country, he said, and wondered if I would let him store it with me.

I refused, of course; he rented one of those places, those timed rental places, and when the storage company flooded in the intervening years, some of those pictures came to the attention of the company management, and Neal was arrested when he came home just a few years later on charges of illegal distribution of whatever across whatever. I believe he is serving twenty years in the Atlanta federal penitentiary or something equally ruinous. I think of him often, standing beside the slide projector, his gaze sliding over some naked twelve-year-old who looks blankly into the camera as if she has no idea what it is.

Connie's face reminded me of those pictures of those girls—not just the first time I saw her, but every time. The look on her face, so blank and frightened. The sense of a vulnerable animal, a spirit barely flickering.

Randall I met five years ago at Covenant House when I went to visit my sister Marie, who worked there writing grants for special programs. Most likely, we had speculated, she got the job because her name was Marie and they believed she was a lapsed Catholic; she had claimed that on her job application and no one ever tried to find out how young she had been when the lapse occurred. Ours was a family of regular Presbyterians, but when I visited Marie I tried to exude the aura of a Catholic, which I pictured as a moist, richly scented cloud of guilt that hung invisibly around me. With this as my meditation, I visited Marie and passed a lounge where a young man was sitting with his legs spread wide.

He only needed one look at me to know me, and when I stood in Marie's office door, he hung out in the waiting room, or whatever kind of room that was, and watched. I was dressed in nice trousers and a mock turtleneck of black cashmere. I was wearing a ruby ring, a gold watch, a gold bracelet, and my ear was pierced with a gold hoop. My shoes shone, and I knew that the aura I exuded was one of a state of constant prosperity. Marie was telling me she had lost eight pounds in the last month and wanted to know if I could see it and lifted her arms like the Madonna, and I said, "Yes, your face looks thinner." When I left the room, the building, and waited at the street corner for the light to change so I could cross to the parking deck and get my car, Randall walked up to me and said, "I just got into town and I was looking for a place to stay back there. But I have a feeling you have a room."

"You do?"

He nodded. "And I want to stay in it. All I have to do is get you to trust me. So what do I do?"

He stood there. Twisted grin and all. Black hair, like mine used to be, straight and thick. The kind of eyes that can make a sucker out of nearly anybody, liquid brown and dark lashed, luxurious and languid, mocking themselves.

"We could have breakfast," I said.

"It's lunchtime," he answered, and the light changed and we walked across to my car. So we had lunch and he told me about himself, since that was what was expected, that he was twenty-two years old, that he came from someplace nobody ever heard of in Mississippi, that most of his family was gone or worthless and no-account; but he did have a sister he loved a lot, though she had a weight problem. He had stayed at home after he got out of high school to work in the Black and Decker factory. But he wanted to strike out in the city. He was looking for somebody to teach him how to live. He said that so simply I had to take another look at him. He had hardly any Southern accent so I suspected he might be lying, though I never said anything. After all that talking I felt obliged to take him home and he stayed there, after that. Forever and ever.

When he got back from taking Connie to the place she lived, a kind of halfway house for special-needs people, he sat me down and told me how he met her.

He had been volunteering with a lesbian friend of ours, Sylvia Norris, to teach an aerobics class, and, while I had known that part, as it turned out he had decided not to tell me that the class was at a place called Green Gardens Assisted Care Home. Connie was in the aerobics class. He described how she had begun class sitting on her heels in a corner, and how it had happened that, slowly, over the course of the hour, repeated day after day, he had drawn her out of herself, teaching her the steps, the up-the-stair-down-the-stair one that makes my knees ache, the leg raises, the shimmy of the hips, all those moves those aerobicists do. Randall loves that kind of thing, moving and sweating, wearing tight clothes, letting people look at him; at least, that was all I saw in it when I tried a class—not one at the special-needs facility, which I knew nothing about at the time—but before that at a nice little place called the Booty Bar.

At Green Gardens Home, the clients were all learning a skill of some kind, and some of the special-needs people already had jobs. Connie's passion was cleaning, though it was a long time before she told him. She liked to clean, she said, or that was what he repeated to me; I can imagine that Connie said something twisted slightly different from that. "I like cleee," she would say, and lead him to the bathroom and show him how she scrubbed the tub, the sink, the toilet. He was laughing at her at first, he said, and then the thought occurred to him that we could use a maid.

I had no trouble thinking Randall could seduce out of her shell a mildly limited girl born with Down syndrome On any Saturday night you can see all that charm for yourself at Spunky's, without the added emotional involvement required by intimacy, without knowing him to have a tender streak, a weakness, for people who need him. Not people who fake a need for him, as I've tried to do from time to time. On Saturday night he's hard, smooth, shaved clean of most feeling, he is a pulse of disco music sliding along the neon of the bar, he is a moment when he strips the shirt over his head and spins around to show his splendid skin, his tight waist, his youth, his treasures. At Spunky's you can look but not touch unless you tip and if you tip maybe you get a sweet little peck on the lips as you slide your fingers down that stiff, smooth chest, wanting to touch that dark brown nipple. At Spunky's I may be sitting somewhere in the room keeping an eye on him, and even if I come without warning I suspect he knows I'm there, but I suspect it's all the same one way or the other; he spins, he takes off his shirt, he slides up and down the bar and makes drinks and kisses men and women on the mouth and sometimes a nice friend takes that nipple and twists it and he purses those lips and backs away. Smooth and hard as a ripple across a pond, a thing you can never gather close in your hand, not to hold it; only a force will work to keep something like that in orbit, a force like gravity, or beauty, or money.

I took him for the interview to get that job at the bar, early one morning the year after he moved in with me. He wanted to get a job in general, at first, and then he wanted to get a job there, and he took me there, or cajoled me into taking him there, night after night to watch the bartenders dance up and down, the bar packed with admirers that had only to watch the show and one another to pass a pleasant evening. I had a friend who knew the owner and I made a call. By then half the town knew Randall was with me anyway and my friends breathed a sigh of relief when they found out he was looking for a job. But when they heard what kind of job he wanted, they assured me, everyone, that I was playing the old fool again. Because the minute he got a job at Spunky's he would be the hottest item imaginable and someone would steal him away from me.

He dressed for the interview in a nice cotton shirt, white, starched, open at the throat, amazing in contrast to the color of his skin. I let him out at the front of the bar and he rang some kind of a buzzer and a man wearing shades and what appeared to be an Armani suit opened the door for him. This was not Ted, the friend of my friend who owned Spunky's, so I pictured him as some kind of bodyguard or shady connection. I parked the car and waited around the corner where there was one of those nouveau silver diners that every city has, these days, in the upscale professional retail part of the town. Something forlorn and sad about the décor, I thought, right down to the gleam of the chrome. Seated on the round red stool at the bar, I ordered the Drive-In Special and a vanilla Coke.

As soon as Randall walked out the door across the street, as soon as all that noonish light hit him, a blaze around him so that even his black hair was shining, I could tell by the jaunt in his walk he had the job. He joined me in the diner and picked up a piece of broccoli from my plate. I could hear it snap as Randall bit it. He was pleased with himself.

Connie became a fixture on Mondays, the day off that Randall could count on. He had me wake him at nine as I was leaving for my first appointment, and on those days, unlike any other, he sat up at once, rubbed his eyes like a boy scout in the woods, and slid out of bed without complaint.

When Connie cleaned a room, she started at one end of it and scrubbed, under that intense scrutiny, one object at a time, until she moved to the other end of the room, and then she was done. In Connie's pattern of movement, a floor was one object, though it had to be cleaned in several ways; but a toilet was a top, a tank, a handle, a lid, a seat, a bowl, and a base. Each object separate, cleaned on every side and polished, whether that made any difference or not. Starting at the top and working down to the bottom.

She cleaned each room of the apartment in order, starting upstairs in one corner in the bedroom and moving methodically through the bathroom, the hall, the guest bath, the two guest rooms, the stairs, the foyer, the living room, the dining room, the little hallway, the laundry room, the breakfast room with the door to the deck, and finally the kitchen, where she ended her day, washing the kitchen cabinets top to bottom and then the counters, all the separate parts of the sink, the fronts of the dishwasher, the refrigerator, the microwave oven, the mini-stereo system, the tiny television bolted under the cabinets, the front of the VCR hidden in the cabinet above the TV, there for when I had to play one of my cooking tapes. At times she dusted and replaced every item in the cabinets as well.

Over the first weeks, a miracle took place, and in the interval from Monday to Monday Randall no longer threw his underwear hither, thither, and yon. In fact, he began to scold me for my habits, leaving dishes in the sink and the like, so that poor Connie would find the place in a mess when she came.

"But that's what we pay her for, dear," I said. "We pay her to come and find the place in a mess and clean it up."

"But she only comes once a week."

"Your point being?"

"It's not fair to make her clean up a week's worth of mess in the kitchen."

"Randall, I am not going to start cleaning up the apartment because the maid is coming over."

He became so angry he shivered and his eyes glazed over. I had never seen this reaction in him before. His hands balled to fists and the color actually drained away from him, as if the contemplation of some truly evil action had caused his Caucasian inheritance to force its way forward. I had the feeling the top of his head might pop off at any second. "Maybe she should come twice a week," I said, and the words dropped right out of my mouth into the place where words go when they are the exact perfect fit for that instant. He could not have induced me to say anything more to his liking.

"For half a day, maybe," I hurried to add.

He appeared to have heard my caveat but he was satisfied and turned away. At that moment, for the first time, I felt jealous of Connie.

For weeks and weeks we went through that same routine. She came on Mondays and cleaned all day, and Randall was always there, picking her up, taking her home. She came again on Fridays in the morning, and Randall was always attentive, always careful. More and more, I dropped in and out of the house to keep an eye on them both.

A man my age should know better than to be jealous in that way. He had been having casual sex with other men his own age for years and I never bothered much about that. Years ago, that first morning Randall was with me, after I knew for sure he was telling the truth, that he really was twenty-two years old and could do what he pleased, including take an old man to bed, he carefully laid out the whole deal. He had showed me his driver's license but I told him I thought that was fake, that I wasn't about to go to bed with any seventeen year old, so he called his sister in Florida and

had her tell me his birthday and of course it could easily not have
been his sister, it could have been anybody, but she said the same
birthday he had told me, including the year, and she told me he always had a baby face, and who was I, and was I good enough for
her brother?

I woke up the next morning and made breakfast for both of
us, tried something complicated in the kitchen and muddled it, and
he laughed at me and I got sensitive, and he laughed at that and I
shut up. He ranged over the apartment as though he already owned
it. At breakfast he proposed his deal. He would sleep with me as
long as he liked it, and he figured he would like it for a pretty long
time unless I hassled him. He would live with me if I wanted him
around. He would do other things that he wanted to do in other
places with other people and he would make sure I never knew what
they were or when they happened. He would be discreet. When he
did have sex with other men he would have safe sex. He would be
tested as often as I liked to make sure he was clean, but he would
expect me to do the same.

I got lost at moments in the melody of his voice, the flute notes
above and below the words. But I understood what he was saying
and I was, after all, forty-five years old at the time. Living alone was
tedious and there was really never any question that I was going to
say no; he understood that and so did I. He was simply laying out
his terms and I had only to take them in. This was, in fact, exactly
what I wanted, too; at least I told myself so. Even if it were not
true, I would have told myself so, at the time, but I do think it was
true, that the deal he proposed was to my liking.

He had two suitcases at the airport in a locker and he wanted me to take him in my car to get them. I broke my first appointment that morning and did exactly what he asked.

I talk to his sister on occasion. She lives in Tallahassee and threatens to visit from time to time, but Randall swears she never will, that she hardly weighs ninety pounds by now and is terrified to go out of the house because of spirit voices overhead. Her husband takes care of her and prays with her at night. Randall has more family in Mississippi on the coast, somewhere along Route 98. I know that much because he mentioned it. I know his mother is still alive and his father is not. As far as I can tell he's an only son, though sometimes I wonder whether he might have a brother. On these subjects he is silent, and if he ever calls his mother, or if she ever calls him, I am never around to hear.

"As far as I am concerned," he tells me, "I can't remember anything further back than walking into the Covenant House and seeing you."

I have wanted to point out to him that he would have to remember at least as far back as putting his suitcases in the locker at the airport and then looking up the address of the Covenant House in a phone book, but he hates to be caught in a mistake.

Connie came from a family who wished to remain anonymous, according to Mrs. Jeter the case worker at the special-needs house, though Connie's last name was listed as Worth. Randall had asked Mrs. Jeter, whom I, too, was destined to meet, about Connie's background. Connie got support to live at the special-needs house from a Catholic charity, which led me to suspect she was from a Catholic family, but her background was as mysterious, in its way, as Randall's. The social workers and case workers at the home were happy to see her employed since she could then pay part of her room and board. She would never, they said, be able to live in an unassisted situation, and her family was not likely to want her back.

Connie fell more deeply in love with Randall over time, and I saw it, but he was oblivious. He needed to think she was immune to that, I guess, to think that those female parts of Connie didn't actually exist. One day, after a full schedule of clients, one of those rare days when I overbooked, I finished the afternoon by showing a house in East Lake, a neighborhood that's been booming with no sign of letup for ten years. That was a hot July day when there'd been no rain for weeks and the front yard of the house crunched stiff and brown. Showing the house proved to be pointless. The right number of bedrooms, but one of them was in the basement and that wouldn't do for a family with two small children, too young for sleeping down there, the mother said. They did have a dog and they were glad the yard was at least already fenced, she could feel safe with the children in the yard because of the fence; I had an image of the children tethered to the fence, cute young dark-eyed things, a nervous mother with a sharp chin, Rhonda or Rhoda, one of the two, Goldberg or Golden, one of the two, and her husband Jay, tall, thin, and bladelike at the nose. The children would love the yard, she kept saying, except we'll never buy this house. The Golden children darted around the rooms and the family kept looking in the closets over and over again. As I recall they did end up buying a house in the Toco Hills area in the nice Jewish neighborhood there, so whatever. That hot afternoon they were not happy with the house I was showing and I was not happy with the heat and when everything was over I went home.

Connie had already reached the dining room in her cleaning itinerary; this was her full day on Monday. As always, when I came in the house, she looked at me and then away, in such a hurry about looking away, and with something in her eyes that had always before made me believe she was afraid of me.

Randall was in the kitchen and gave me a peck on the lips, and I happened to be glancing in Connie's direction, and she glanced at me again, her black eyes for the moment full of malice. She hurriedly looked away as before, but the feelings moved slowly across her face. I realized at that moment she had hated me, too, all this time.

"Ran," she said, with an audible break in her voice, and turned away and walked into the laundry room.

"What, Connie, sweetie?" he asked, and hurried to find her.

I poured myself a scotch from the twenty-six-year-old bottle that I keep for afternoons when the Atlanta real estate market seems too much to bear. I carried my heavy crystal glass to the deck, where I sat under the raised umbrella and looked out over Piedmont Park.

Later, when he returned from driving her home, he appeared shaken, and he disappeared into the bedroom before wandering through the rooms turning on lamps, as he always does as soon as dusk descends. He has a horror of a dark room. I watched him in the living room standing over the red lacquer lamp painted with the Chinese ideograms for health, happiness, and prosperity. He must have seen my shadow through the glass because he moved through the rooms toward me and I could see a flickering of need in his eyes, of confusion certainly, but of something else, of trust

and need, and these were for me, were my part of him, and I remembered, suddenly, his five-years-younger face looking at me and
saying, "All I have to do is get you to trust me. What do I do?"

But I had only a moment to realize how happy I had become
before he sat down and said, "Connie started crying in the car and
wouldn't stop."

"Crying?"

"Yes." He shook his head. "She was trying to say something but
I couldn't figure out what it was. I've never seen her like that. It
shook me up, and the case worker saw her. She thought something
was wrong, too."

"Connie's in love with you," I said.

"Cut it out, this is serious."

"Randall," I said, "I know it is. And I know I'm right. She's in
love with you."

He looked at me a long time, shock spreading across his face.
"You really think she is?"

"You're nice to her. That's all it takes. How would she know
any better?"

He sat back. He saw my scotch and wanted one but never so
much as raised his hand. I went to fetch it and brought it to him
and left him there to think.

He went away preoccupied and I started dinner and for just a
moment, not even for a moment, really, the flickering of my hatred
for Connie stirred and I wondered if I had told him so glibly that
she loved him out of malice. I wondered if I had done anything
wrong, by doing that. Because I could see this news would change
Randall's relations with her; and I was puzzled at myself, at the note

of glee in the undercurrents of me, as I unwrapped the chicken breasts stuffed with goat cheese and sun-dried tomato that I had picked up from Harry's in a Hurry.

I put together a quick salad and warmed the chicken. He would hear me making his dinner; as always. I ate with him and watched him. His color had changed; he seemed drawn. I understood then that Connie had never been real to him. She had been a good deed to do, a person he could help, not a woman with a body who would respond to his good looks. He had thought he was safe with her.

Through the whole meal I could see the question on his face.

When I was bringing out the espresso, he did say, "You think everybody's in love with me."

"Nearly everybody is, dear," I said, pretending to be blithe for a moment.

The words sank over him like a weight. He pushed back his chair, drank the espresso in one gulp, exactly like an old Italian I had seen once in a café in Milano. Poured it straight down his throat.

In a moment I heard him walking with his car keys and the next thing I knew he was standing in the kitchen, while I moved past him clearing the table. "I'm going out," he said. "I'll be late."

"Oh?"

He was already at the back door. Gone. I listened to the jingle of his keys and him on the stairs and then I stopped listening.

What was the expression on his face? Why couldn't I recognize it? Hadn't I seen all his expressions before?

I tried to read a Stephen Frye novel that I had bought months before but none of the words would stick together. I watered the plants. I spread out newspaper on the kitchen floor and repotted a fern that was getting root-bound. Something sensual about tearing at the tight packed roots, pulling them free so they would grow out into the new soil in the new pot.

He had gone to the clubs. I had almost a vision, him walking to a house that looked empty, the windows white from the outside, and inside, young men everywhere, patrons of Spunky's, boys from the A list all over town, low lights, hard loud music, a room with a bar and a room for drugs, those designer things that he takes, from time to time, but that I decline to use. He is wearing less and less clothing as he walks farther into the house. Soon he's in a room that's teeming with men, slithering and sliding over and over one another, like the back room of the Bourbon Pub in the French Quarter of New Orleans on almost any night in 1978 when I was there. His orgies became my orgies and they all blended in my mind. It was as if he had gone out that night to visit my past.

In my room in a book that Randall was not likely ever to open, a copy of *À la recherche du temps perdu* meant to impress people and to provide a convenient hiding place for travelers checks, I keep a picture Neal Crook gave me the last time we were together. He had come back from Morocco and called me and I thought he wanted to buy a house. But it turned out he had been arrested for possession of that huge collection of child pornography and what he wanted was help with renting a place since he figured to be going to prison in a few months.

He came to the office one afternoon. For the first time in memory he was wearing neither ascot nor tie but simply a white cotton shirt, the button open at the collar. He told me what had happened and I was stunned, and I remembered my own refusal to hide the stuff for him, and for a moment I wished I had said yes. I had been reviewing some new listings I had pulled off the computer but closed the folder and said, "I'm very sorry."

"Oh, no need for that. I knew I was running the risk."

I asked him to give me the phone number of his hotel—he had only been back in the country a few days and had been arrested almost immediately upon presenting himself at the storage company, which had sent him a bland letter about the flood damage. He wrote the number on the back of a picture he was carrying in his pocket and I told him I would get a good leasing agent to call him as soon as I could find one. He thanked me and laid the picture face down on the desk, to show the number, I thought. "The picture is a little gift," he said. "In case you think I'm the least bit repentant."

A Polaroid of a young girl, nude, exactly like all the others he had shown me in his apartment that was soon to become mine, years ago. Nipples swollen, nascent breasts pushing gently beneath the skin. A look on her face so blank it seemed there was nothing behind her eyes at all.

He smiled, and stood. "That's my last one," he said. "The very last picture I own."

"Well. Thank you, I guess."

He bowed his head and left.

That was the picture I had placed years ago in the Proust volume and I took it out now to study it. I had the feeling it would turn out to be Connie's face, somehow, that some impossible coincidence like that would take place, and all the threads of this would come together. A pale, poorly lit, pudgy girl with mottled skin and dark, dank curls, a soft lower belly and broad hips, a vulva so tender and unformed it looked like an unbaked dinner roll, threads of soft dark hair.

Two days later, the case worker, Mrs. Jeter, visited us in the late afternoon. She left a card with us and I have read her first name at least a hundred times since, but I can never remember it unless I'm looking at it. Randall had taken her call and told me just before she was arriving that he expected a visit. She trundled into the apartment from the front parking spaces, large hips rolling under the stretch skirt, a purse and a large leather carryall bag looped over one shoulder. Randall stood to the side to let her pass and I stepped back into the kitchen. They were already talking by the time they came into earshot.

"She upset, all right," Mrs. Jeter said, and sat on the couch, blowing out a big breath and piling her bags like a fortress wall onto the cushions beside her. "She got a good reason to be, son. She pregnant."

I could have heard a pin drop inside myself. My own shock was so complete I have no idea how Randall reacted. I walked to the edge of the living room and Mrs. Jeter saw me and nodded pleasantly. "How do?" she asked.

"Hello. Would you care for anything to drink?"

Randall introduced us. Mrs. Jeter said, "Thank you for having me into your home, Mr. Hyde, and I'd appreciate a nice glass of cool water with no ice." Touching the folds of her neck delicately with the corner of a kerchief.

Randall asked, "Does she know? Does she understand?"

"Sometimes she understands a little," Mrs. Jeter said. "Other times she just cry because her stomach feels funny."

"When did you find out?" Randall asked.

"The doctor let us know a couple of days ago." By then I was in the kitchen and had no idea what her expression was. Her voice carried a ring of expectancy. "She says the child is yours, when she realizes we're talking about a baby. She says you're the daddy."

"Mrs. Jeter, I assure you—I'm gay, I live here with Henry. I've had nothing at all to do with Connie that way."

I had come to the door and was looking at him when he said it. My heart had stopped when I realized what Mrs. Jeter was here to ask, but when I saw his face, I knew he was telling the truth.

"I had a feeling that was what you were going to tell me." Mrs. Jeter accepted the glass of water from me with a gracious dip of the head.

"You did?" he asked.

"Oh, yes." She waved her hand. "She's truly simple in her mind, Randall. I would expect her to name you as the daddy of the baby. It's hardly even real in her mind, the connection between whatever happened to her and the child."

"Then who?" he asked, so quietly.

"The first person I would suspect would be somebody on staff, but as it happens, just at the moment, there aren't any men working with us." She drank deeply from the glass of water and looked around at the living room. Handing me the glass, struggling to rise, she said, "Well, I've wasted enough of you people's time."

"But what about Connie?"

She had reached her feet and stood stock still, solid, as if she had grown roots there. "It's a sad mess," she said. "Her daddy come to see her about a month ago. I believe this is her daddy's child."

Tears in Randall's eyes. Such a sudden rush. I looked away.

"Well," she sighed, "let me go."

"What's going to happen to her?"

"We'll take care of Constance," Mrs. Jeter said. "Some way. Don't you worry." She sighed. She looked at us both. "But I don't think she should come back here any more."

Randall sat on the deck a long time by himself, dry eyed and calm.

The first morning we were ever together, when we had made love very sweetly and I understood how thoughtful he was, I already knew he would never love me very much, but that he would never love me any less than that. How do you describe the instinct that you have about a man after you have made those necessary visits inside one another? How do you know you know? I understood that he would stay for a long time, that he would never care for me more than was comfortable, that he would always be discreet when he was seeing someone else, that he would love me quite faithfully from a fixed orbit, a dependable moon of affection. I had understood I had no power ever to break his heart and that this was the reason he had felt completely safe with me; I was frightened that he had understood so much about me in such a little time; but I was willing to take the chance, and time has proved me right.

It took Connie to break his heart. Even as miserable and wretched as she was, I couldn't help but hate her more, when I understood that.

A few nights later I go to Spunky's. It is a Saturday night, everybody is out, everybody is there. I have come to the bar to lurk along the walls out of sight. I am wearing tinted glasses that give the disco lights an alien cast, and the pulse of the music throbs so heavy with bass that my bones are shivering in the sound waves. From a distance I see Randall, stripped down to his white cotton Calvin T-shirt, the soft cloth exactly right across his shoulders, the pure white against his red-toned skin, those black eyes drinking everything around them, and him all rhythm and motion, twirling and gliding, bending forward to hear some drink order, some whispered flirtation, some never-mind-what. I look for some change in him that registers here, in these wavelengths of his life, but out here he is all performance; out here nothing touches him.

Still, one moment, when he knows I'm here, when he catches my eye across the bar, there is a softness, a place between us that was never there before. I only want to feel it for a moment, no longer. I can't contain it more than that. It is the purest feeling of an open space, a wind blowing brush across a plain, and then it vanishes and he twists away.

HOUSE
ON THE EDGE

IN the dream, alone in a room, I lie under blankets that seem heavy and protective, though they are only wool. The bed is narrow, and sags in the middle. I lie with my torso half-turned, uncomfortable, wanting to move—but I have stopped still. I listen.

I can feel the whole house around me, rising a hundred floors above and descending a hundred below, so that I share in equal parts the house's emptiness and weight. I hope I am alone here. Maybe he has not come tonight, maybe the halls are only full of crying wind, maybe that is what I hear. If I could go to the door I know what I would see. A wide corridor runs down one way and turns, and runs down the other way and turns, so that the door to my room is in the middle, the only door here. The corridor sags with heavy darkness. Night lights line the walls, but the bulbs burned out long ago; never replaced, since rats have chewed so many wires in pieces we have no more electricity. Maybe it's rats I hear running in the halls now, their feet making noise on the floor, whispering noise that only seems like a voice.

No. Now the voice comes again, undeniable. "Daniel," the voice calls sharp and clear, "Daniel, let me in." The voice has teeth that rake my spine. I grow rigid, cannot even breathe, cannot hear his breathing; but he is there, all the same.

I can't lie in this position any more, I have to move. But if I do the mattress will creak. I go slowly, ease against the wall, cool to my skin; but when I try to move my legs the mattress springs shriek, and I close my eyes. He whispers "Daniel, Daniel." He rattles the doorknob, I hold still, and breathe, quietly. He leans close to the door, and runs his hands along it. His palms make sucking noises against the wood. I watch the door, certain I have locked it. Here one always locks one's door at night.

There are parts of the dream that are only hinted. I am something other than human here. Though I never leave my room, I can actually see outside it, as if I contain two sorts of vision—the first specific, applying only to the room; the other general, like the movie camera that sweeps over city skyscrapers to isolate one bare window. I can feel the air dropping away from my window, even though the windows here don't open: it is as if I hang in the air and see, beyond, gray shapes that can only be mountains, a smooth gray sky, gray clouds and mists. But this building is too enormous to see all at once, a wall of rock, absorbing all sunlight. Bleak snow covers the roof. In the dream, it is always night. During the day though, what do I do? Do I ever leave the room? Do I walk the empty halls, do I go into other rooms, turn over dusty magazines, finger the fringes of some lamp not touched in maybe a hundred years? No.

No, these are wrong. During the day I roam. The house is vast, is on the edge of something. I long to get out, I search, I try for exits but find only corridors, endless stairways, rows of bare windows that won't open. I long for the fresh air from outside.

In the dream, I can never stay in the same room for long. He always finds me. Sometimes I rest whole nights, never having to wake; but always waiting, always on the edge, knowing he roams the halls, listening, smelling under the doors, knowing one night soon he'll be at my door again, calling my name. Tonight he has found me again, tonight he calls over and over "Daniel;" rattling the doors, "Daniel;" running his nails along the wood, "Daniel, Daniel;" pressing his lips against the crack in the door, so his words are distorted. I close my eyes, pretend not to hear. Once I try to call out, but no sound will come; none can pass the deep weight in my chest that is part of his magic. I only make low animal noises, soft moanings and other aching rushes of air.

He starts to pick the lock. He doesn't tell me what he is doing, but I can hear. A thin metal wire goes in, clicking against the tumblers. Click, click, click, he pushes, shoves, fingers the lock with the wire. Now his breath comes ragged. The first time he ever tried to pick a lock in a room where I slept, I was dreaming the dream: the halls teemed with invisible men and women, none of whom could see one another, all fleeing from the same man. I woke to the sound of scratching, and thought the door was swinging open. I tried to scream, arching upward with the urge to make sound. But still no sound would come.

Even if I make noise, nothing will change. No one is here. The house is all waste. Some disaster has happened, some war perhaps, and all the lower floors are ruin. I know that below a certain point none of the doors open any more. The house is a desert of rooms, and even I, who know it best, don't know how wide it is. Though I heard once, when people still lived here, that the halls all run in a wide circle, that there really is only a single hall, running upward in a spiral so vast that one can feel neither the curve nor the grade. Maybe I believe that tonight. Sometimes I feel the emptiness emanating like a poisonous gas from the rooms. Or sometimes I can feel the wind get in through a hole somewhere, and look for it, but never find it. Somewhere above is a gash in the outer wall a hundred yards wide. I saw it years ago. If I could get back there now I would jump out of it, but I might wander here for years and never find it. The house shifts its shape at night, the house is shaped like wind. I still would rather live than die, at least during the day. At least then he leaves me alone.

Though maybe some day he won't. Maybe when I open my room to go out he'll still be there one morning. Maybe that will put an end to all this running. But I can't hope for that. If dying is what I want, I ought to kill myself—cut open my arm on some broken vase and watch the life spill away—not wait for him to do it. He'll be gone this morning, same as any other. Unless he gets in tonight. Then it won't matter any more. A long time ago some people here told me about him, back when the building first began to empty. Faces would stop me in the hall and voices would say gravely that Something walks at night in the emptying upper floors, Something not human. First a woman was found with her neck open. Then it got worse. Two or three died every night, and people began buying elaborate locks for their doors. Those are the rooms I look for now, the rooms where frightened people lived, where whole lines of locks bar each exit, as many as a dozen to a door. Up at the top there are lots of rooms like those, and if I had stayed on the highest floors, I don't think he would ever have reached me. Even the walker can't pick a dozen locks all at once.

I don't know who he is, I've never seen his face. Sometimes I think he looks like my father, though that is only my imagination. Once I saw his feet, one night when, brave, I peeped under the door to see if he was real. He smelled how close I was, and rattled the door like thunder. I thought it would break in. His feet were bare, white as snow, and the toenails were ragged, gray. I don't know where he comes from, or what he does during the day. I don't know where he learned my name. Tonight I only know one thing, really. I've made a mistake, coming to this room. It's too far down, only one lock bars the door, and I hear the wire whispering to it. After a long time the first tumbler falls, a soft, rolling noise. I lie flat, the blankets now so heavy I can't breathe. "Daniel," he says low, "Hello Daniel; Hello Daniel."

The second tumbler falls faster. He chuckles. I can hear him sniffing. He pushes the door against its frame and laughs again. "Are you scared, Danny? Would I hurt the pretty Dan? Would I cut his pretty throat? Would I?"

I shake my head, my throat still closed. This is a dream. The third tumbler falls and I become frantic, my heart almost bursts out of my ribs; I lie flat on the bed, heavy, unmoving, the blankets in a ring around my neck, I swim under heavy water; and when the fourth tumbler goes I do scream, my throat begrudging me those aching hoarse screams that sleeping people scream; the door begins to open and I see him at last.

Here I wake. Sometimes my roommate has heard me, and comes to the door. "Are you all right?" he asks.

"I don't know," I say out of sleep; and then, more conscious of myself, "Yes, I'm all right."

He nods. For him it is enough that I answer. Watching him, sharing nothing, I wonder why I cannot move. My roommate closes the door.

But there are times yet worse, times like tonight, when the dream door swinging open is my own, when the empty house I wake into is this one. I can see him at the door, his blue eyes glowing—this is not a dream any more, but I can still see him, can even hear his breath, heavy and forced. For a long time he looks at me. But at the end he only smiles, derisive. Something is not finished between us. He turns away, as if to say you are no good to me dead. I hold still against the pillow, listening to the house. If I hear a noise, I'm afraid of the noise; if I hear nothing, I'm afraid of the nothing. I tell myself I am all right. Sometimes I lie still a long time after waking, before I even dare to turn on a light. Then I find paper, and write a letter to a friend, write Bible verses, write this dream even, until the sun rises and I can search the house safely, to make certain no one is there.

STANLEY
KARENINA

HAPPY marriages are all alike. Each unhappy marriage is unhappy in its own way.

When Stanley married Bob, swearing before God to love, honor, and obey, until death do them part, they were each as sincere as men can be. Men, gay or straight, always are sincere to the best of their abilities, which often are not great.

When marrying Stanley, Bob felt completely convinced that he was on the right path, finally, after a lot of waffling and hiding from himself. Bob had met someone whom he felt he could love forever. Like so many people, Bob had felt this way before.

For instance, Bob had been completely convinced of his own correctness when he married Irene right after college, too. He would come to think of Irene as his first wife, and Stanley as his second. He married Irene in a Methodist Church and Stanley in a Unitarian Fellowship Center. In neither of Bob's marriages was he the write-your-own-vows type. He liked the standard words that he had heard all his life on television and in the movies. But when he married Irene, he didn't know he was gay. Or he knew, and he pretended it would go away, like a prolonged head cold. So later he would think that his marriage to Irene did not really count.

Stanley had never been married. He had been too aware of the tragic consequences of a bad choice, such as the death of Anna Karenina. He had longed for a love for which he would fling himself under a train without a second thought, but only when he met Bob did he feel such a stirring. Bob being married, at first Stanley decided this feeling was the recurrence of his old need for approval from straight men, the issue that had kept him in years of group therapy. The two men met at a racetrack. Bob introduced himself to Stanley while they stood in line to bet on a filly ridden by a Russian jockey. The odds were long, ten to one or more. The filly broke her leg on the homestretch. Bob and Stanley were watching each other as the horse collapsed on the track, shuddering and heaving in the dry red dirt. Bob signaled to Stanley and they walked away together.

Which kind of marriage is the sacred one, the kind Bob had to Irene or the kind Bob had with Stanley?

When Bob was married to Irene, she thought they had a pretty good sex life. A pretty good sex life was all she wanted. Neither of them had ever been enthusiastic about copulation, even in college. They made a kind of silent agreement to have sex in private in order for the knowledge of these fumblings to make them feel more comfortable in other social settings, where it was helpful no longer to be virgins. They attempted to enjoy their activities but mostly finished as quickly as possible. By the time they were married they had grown used to having sex on occasion and even enjoying it, though Irene's orgasms often frightened Bob.

Stanley and Bob, after a frightening amount of intercourse in the early months of their relationship, settled down to much the same pattern.

Bob had cheated on Irene a number of times during their years together and never told her about any of the times this happened, and never gotten caught. He chose both men and women for his betrayals. Far from cleaving only unto Irene, he cleaved unto almost anybody he met.

When Bob and Stanley got married, however, Stanley was the first to cheat. He did an old boyfriend in the bathroom during the wedding reception. Later he would tell himself he did it because he was frightened of commitment.

Both Irene and Stanley were scarred by the divorces of their own parents, though they never discussed this with one another the few times they actually met. Bob came from a marriage that lasted fifty years, marked by the fact that neither parent would leave the company of the other and that neither parent ever spoke to the other except to fill the most basic of needs, such as locating the remote control for the television or discussing another vacation trip to Helen, Georgia.

Irene and Stanley had issues about faith and constancy that lasted through most of their lives. In fact, they were very similar as people and, had Stanley been heterosexual, they might have become attracted to one another and married each other successfully. But they both married Bob.

Bob was short. Irene and Stanley were tall.

Bob never actually divorced Irene and never actually stopped sleeping with her. He was incapable of constancy and had a compulsion to prove it. He moved in with Stanley and later had a wedding with Stanley but he was always actually married to Irene.

Picture the scene when Stanley finds this out. Worthy of a Russian novel, if it were to occur on the North American continent, it ought to be set in a mountainside inn on a snowy evening outside Montreal. Bob stumbles forward into the inn, having come from a visit to Irene, sick with consumption, coughing blood quietly into her bread, in a cabin in the deep mountains with snow falling in bales. Stanley receives Bob coldly and demands to know where he has been. Bob, agitated, spills the whole tale, his refusal to divorce Irene out of weakness, his act of betrayal in marrying Stanley, an act merely heinous and not at all illegal since any gay marriage means spit in this country.

Bob and Stanley have a child, an African-American daughter they adopted from an unwed teenager in South Carolina. In fact only one of them is the legally adoptive parent but they are understandably reluctant to admit which of them it is. Stanley dotes on his daughter, and believes she will attend Princeton or even Emory and will someday win a Rhodes Scholarship. He thinks that winning the Rhodes scholarship would be the pinnacle of a person's life, and the culmination of any parent's dream.

Irene has a child who is not Bob's but someone else's, a child from her high school days who was put up for adoption. After years of searching, and et cetera, the child found her mother. This girl's name is Roberta and for a while she was convinced that Bob was her father and was hiding the fact from her, which made her understandably angry, though it was not, of course, true. Roberta got along well with Stanley, with whom she was certain she shared no kinship at all.

Which of these people is most likely to hurl himself or herself under a train on a wintry night in Moscow? Due to having violated the most sacred of human bonds? What indelible connection actually exists between any of these people?

Bob's parents, on their fifty-first wedding anniversary, invite Irene and Stanley to the party, and each is treated with equal intimacy, to the point that a visitor might have thought it was Irene and Stanley who were members of the family and Bob who was the outsider.

The end of the evening is the usual look through Bob's parents' wedding pictures, with the old-fashioned photographs of the old-style wedding getups, everything posed and arranged symmetrically in front of the most sacred spot known to American man, the pulpit of the Baptist church, from which God blessed this union.

Irene and Stanley are both thinking about their weddings to Bob, and wondering why Bob's parents, in their wedding photographs, appear so much more substantial.

These more or less congenial scenes all occur before Stanley learns that Bob never actually divorced Irene. When Stanley does learn this, he becomes deeply depressed, and burns the master copy of the videotape of his own wedding, which was really only a commitment ceremony, taking place in the local Unitarian Church. Which, as everyone knows, is not a real church at all.

Were this the nineteenth century and were Stanley about to take a long journey by train, he might consider throwing himself under the wheels after Bob's revelation. Stanley would take this step not with a conscious decision but would move toward it irrevocably moment by moment, so that even a person who knew him well, even he himself, would not understand until the very last second that he was about to put an end to himself.

But this is the twenty-first century. He could drive his car into a tree but his airbags might well save him. He might try to hurl himself under the wheels of a passenger jet as it wheeled back from the jetway, but he would probably be arrested as a potential terrorist before he ever got near those huge head-squashing tires. As for using an actual train, the Amtrak schedule through Atlanta is simply too eccentric, and there is never snow.

If someone were explaining Stanley's suicide to someone else, as the result of a broken vow, the person to whom all this was being explained would simply be irritated that Stanley did not get over his little trauma and move on.

Stanley will always feel married to Bob. He has never been married to anybody else, and never will be.

Irene will always feel married to Bob. She met him when she was just a girl. He was her first—no, her second—no, her third?—true love.

Bob will never really feel married to anybody. He has never been capable of such attachment, and never will be.

Marriage is a sacred state when there is some degree of the sacred involved in its making. The legal state cannot make any such institution sacrosanct. In fact, one might argue, the legal state is obligated not to do so.

The church cannot necessarily involve the sacred in joining

any two people together, either, but in the case of the church, one has to see through a good deal of hocus-pocus in order to understand this.

The end of the story is that Stanley leaves Bob eventually, gets counseling, and puts his daughter through college like a good single parent. Stanley dates and has relationships but never again undergoes a marriage-like commitment ceremony with anyone.

Bob starts to call himself bisexual and meets another woman, Betty, who insists on Bob's actually divorcing Irene. Bob marries Betty, after separating himself from the woman to whom, in the eyes of God, he will always be joined, if marriage is a sacred state.

One day Betty finds the photographs of Bob's wedding to Stanley. She thinks it's a joke at first, then she thinks it's not a joke at all. But Bob is her fourth husband, and they are getting along pretty well. So she puts away the wedding album with the photographs of the two men standing side by side, and she pretends she never saw it.

Irene, meanwhile, never marries again after Bob, and lives happily single for the rest of her life. She happened to settle on the same street in Decatur as Stanley. Now and then they stop at one another's yards to talk about their gardens, but they never talk about Bob at all.

9/20/2010

NEW JERUSALEM

to Flannery O'Connor

LOMAX made Mama promise to have a picnic the first spring day that come up good and warm. Mama could devil some eggs and fry some chicken, and Alphonso could set up Lomax's easel and paints by the cow pond. They'd carry some bug spray and a fly swat. Mama fretted about when she would possibly find the time to worry about devilling eggs, with cows in calf and the help to watch every minute. "What they don't wreck they steal," Mama always said. On this occasion she added, "But if you want a picnic I will lay aside my duties and get you one up, the next pretty day."

"It's not as if I won't be right in the kitchen with you," Lomax said.

Mama sighed and clucked her tongue. "I don't know if I would call that help."

Many dairy disasters intervened, and Lomax also sold a picture and had her final visit to the hospital. "I've about decided I know how I'm going to spend my money," Lomax announced, post recovery, on the morning Mama finally decided the weather in-clined toward picnic quality.

"Leave it in the bank," Mama said.

"I'm going to buy me a trip to the moon." Lomax peeled boiled eggs and dropped the shells into a small metal pot. "If what I read here is correct the government will be offering trips up that way soon. And it would be mighty good to be up there where I wouldn't weigh but fifteen pounds. I'll buy me a one-way ticket, you watch."

"You will not do any such of a thing."

"You can come with me if you ain't dead," Lomax said. "I'll buy us two tickets."

"Listen to me, Lomax Lamb," Mama said, swelling up her chest. "Nobody ain't been to the moon and nobody ain't going there."

"Mama, you saw the astronauts standing on the moon just like I did. Right on the television."

"If you believe everything you see on the silver screen you are in sad shape. Them pictures was from a TV studio somewhere." Mama mixed the potato salad with her hands. The wet potatoes made oceanic belches as she rolled them over the chopped celery and onion. She spied Lomax eyeing the red pepper box and said, "If you ruin them devil eggs with that cayenne pepper I will turn you across my knee big as you are. Good as I love a devil egg."

"They got to be hot," Lomax said, and devilled them just as she pleased.

Alphonso carried the painting apparatus. The color of deep tree shadow, Alphonso came up to Lomax's ribs, his body a riot of contained energy as he headed across the pasture. Lomax had to warn him not to drag the canvas through the grass. She followed behind, swinging merrily on her crutches, doing her best to keep up. A leather quiver of paints and brushes swung at her hip, weighing against her cotton dress. In the distance the small herd of Mama's cows lowed and swished flies. Mama had told the Mexican to move them to the east field but Lomax no longer trusted cows to stay where they belonged. She verified the integrity of the fence with careful inspection. Alphonso was singing about how to set his feet on higher ground, and the clear bell tone of his voice put Lomax in a good mood. Mama kept telling Alphonso to go slow and Alphonso answered he was going as slow as he could without plumb dying. Mama waddled through the high grass dragging the picnic basket and thermos full of muttering ice cubes. Once a gust of wind tore the floppy hat with the gauze band off Mama's head, and Alphonso dashed after it, dropping everything. Mama squinted helplessly, and Lomax put her own smaller hat on Mama's head. "There, there," Lomax said, gauging the damage to her canvases and paints as Alphonso leapt like a sprite through the grass.

At the cow pond, Mama told Alphonso, "Miss Lomax is going to fly to the moon. What do you think about that?"

Alphonso squinted at Lomax. He set up the low easel where she could reach it, and spread the flannel blanket for her, beating down the grass. "It's probably some snakes out here," he said.

"You don't believe me, do you?" Lomax demanded.

"How do you plan to get to the moon?" Mama tittered, which meant she had made up a joke. "You got a rocket in your room?"

"I'm buying me a ticket. You watch. I may go today." Lomax lowered herself to the blanket and arranged her paint tubes in a rainbow.

Alphonso said, "Miss Estabelle showed me on her TV where they ain't no moon, they just a big light, and we close to it as we going to get."

"Miss Estabelle don't have a TV," Lomax said.

"Estabelle certainly does have a TV," Mama said, unwrapping a plate of cheese crackers.

"Well, it don't work," Lomax said.

"She says she can see the picture," Mama said.

"Miss Estabelle don't need no TV to show the moon for what it is," Alphonso said, and ran off after a dragonfly. He came back with it cupped in his palms, listening to it and letting Lomax listen, too. The dragonfly hummed a popular radio tune. They both, Lomax and Alphonso, laughed at the same time in the same amazement, but the tune continued, unmistakable. "Miss Estabelle says the dragonfly is the eagle of the insects." Alphonso threw up his hands and the dragonfly burst into Lomax's face. She gasped and sat back.

Alphonso selected the wing and the short leg from the chicken plate. Mama handed Lomax a fried chicken breast, and she ate the chicken with one hand and dabbed paint onto a strip of cardboard with the other.

"I need some potato salad and saccharin tea," Lomax said.

"These eggs are seasoned just right," Mama said. "Mighty good."

"I do not want one word of praise after you hollered at me like you did. This chicken is so dry it ain't even worth mentioning."

"Lomax Lamb, I will knock a knot on you."

Lomax dabbed and stroked. The wind ran across the grass like something alive, and the pulse of it made her stand outside herself, listening from a great distance. The whole canvas of color seemed to arrange itself without any help from her, while she admired the taste of the chicken breast and listened to the wind. Alphonso ran off somewhere again. He might have been dancing in the grass, from the look. Far off beyond the fence, under a grove of shade trees, the cows were grazing. For a while Lomax watched them, partly to admire them and partly to make sure they were staying where they belonged. For a while she watched the frame shacks the help lived in, the Mexican woman in her yard, chickens at her feet. The water of the cow pond translated itself through Lomax's fingers into a patch of eerie aquamarine that shimmered on the canvas. She liked that blue. Pausing, she watched the color and the real water, spooning on potato salad and shoving a whole devil egg in her mouth.

"You eat like a sow," Mama said.

"You never taught me any manners that stuck, so blame yourself if you get disgraced." Lomax licked her fingers for the last bit of cayenne, and purposefully slurped her tea.

"Yonder she comes," Mama said.

Alphonzo ran breathless beside Miss Estabelle along the edge of the cow pond. Miss Estabelle carried her cane and a strand of cattail like a rod and scepter, her dress bleached grey by the sun, holes cut raggedly for her arms and legs, an ample, full garment, rippling in the breeze. Miss Estabelle, who lived in the woods beyond the pasture, had a wide, flaring nose and high, round cheeks, the skin beginning to go slack and hollow beneath. She eased herself down in the grass and folded her hands in her lap. With her calm, mild eyes she studied the picnic blanket, and then turned to Mama. "You brought your little girl into the cow pasture," she said.

Lomax, nearing thirty-four, felt uneasy being called Mama's little girl. She started to say something but Mama gave her the eye. "Yes, I brought her on a picnic out here, after she worried me for a solid month.

"The children got no patience," said Miss Estabelle.

"Is your real name Esther Belle?" Lomax asked, watching the colors of the woman's face and daubing paint with small, nearly invisible gestures.

"I ain't got no name but what the Lord call me." Miss Estabelle made circles in the air with her cane, clean blond wood worn smooth by handling. "But I wish he would call me to the Angels. I'm ready to go."

"Hush that," Mama said. "When here I have fried all this chicken."

"God bless you for a short thigh and some potato salad," said Estabelle politely.

"Mercy, you can eat more than that. Eat some of this slaw. And this ham biscuit."

"God bless you," Miss Estabelle said. "It's not every white woman can fry chicken." She dipped her thin bonnet of hair toward Mama, who gave her a plastic fork and a cup of sugar tea. A bee buzzed around their heads. Alphonso whacked it dead with Lomax's paint palette. The dead bee stuck to the cardboard and Alphonso, fearing the sting of the bee-ghost, refused to remove it. Lomax stuck the corpse to the canvas on a white patch that had begun as a water lily, painted over the dead insect with black and red, the dry paint and sealer preserving the bee for the ages. The others ate and watched Lomax. Alphonso told Miss Estabelle that Miss

Lomax was going to the moon soon. He clapped his hands and laughed. Miss Estabelle said the moon was no place to go, there was a whole sea of storms on it, and nothing would grow.

"I am not of this world," Lomax said, sitting up straight. "I would be right at home there."

"I don't know why she talks like that, I take her to church," said Mama, wiping her mouth between bites of chicken back. "Though God knows I could confess her sins for her if anybody wanted me to."

"Oh hush. Nobody wants you to."

Mama fixed her with a glare.

Miss Estabelle rapped her knuckles. "Honor thy father or thy mother."

"It is a heap easier to honor my father who is dead and gone," Lomax said, in a practical tone. She sat back and studied the canvas. Again she felt the wind come up and heard Alphonso's laugh of delight when it whipped the grass in shadows and waves. Mama and Miss Estabelle were in the midst of agreeing there was no re- spect left among the young. Mama said she never knew what she did to deserve such a worthless daughter, good for nothing but to dab color all over everything and dirty up the sink with paints. Lo- max allowed dryly that this worthless daughter presently brought in a sizable chunk of the family income with them dabs of color, whereas Mama could barely convince a cow to give milk.

Mama harrumphed and bit an egg with too much cayenne.

"This picture is of the pond right here," said Miss Estabelle, pointing, while Mama hurriedly drank a glass of tea.

"How do you know what it is?"

"You got the lily and the water crocuses. You got Alphonso. Why look here. I see what you done. I bet you think that's me, don't you?"

"I don't reckon I ought to say," Lomax purred. "You might try to charge me."

Turning her head this way and that. "Like a sunny day." Estabelle said.

"It's mighty nice of you to notice. My Mama don't appreciate my art until it transfigurizes into dollars."

"You need a cow in it," Mama said. "I like a good picture of a cow."

Miss Estabelle said, "You were wicked to paint that Prophet like you did."

Lomax felt a thrill go up her spine. "When did you see my Prophet?"

"I saw him when I saw him," Miss Estabelle said. "He has been reading the writing on the wall. He has been weighed in the scale and found wanting. His days have been numbered and are brought to an end."

"Is she talking about that ugly picture you got hanging over your dresser?" Mama smeared mayonnaise onto ham biscuit. "Many's the time I've spoilt my appetite looking at that thing."

Miss Estabelle turned to Mama and asked, in a bold voice, "What would you do if you saw somebody's real face struck by the grace light?"

"It's no sense in wondering," Mama said. "Do you want some more sugar tea?"

"Thank you for some," said Miss Estabelle, extending her cup, her arm veined, the soft flesh feathering from the bone. She smiled up into Mama's face. "But you need to know, Mother Lamb. You need to know what to do when you see the Face."

"Lomax will certainly tell me what to do when she sees it," Mama said, and Miss Estabelle shook her head.

Lomax let a little smile occur but went on painting She had rarely felt such conflagration. Afternoon light hung over the pond like liquid amber. Dragonflies swooped in curves and sang, jeweled wings flashing. Alphonso leapt in the grass, bluish light on the planes of his face, his glad self-absorption evident as a thread through a multitude of expressions. Her hand pursued each gleam, slashing with the brush, teasing it, studying the canvas like an adversary. She could hardly make a wrong brushstroke if she tried.

"The handwriting is on the wall," Miss Estabelle said, in a voice meant to reach Lomax. She sipped from her Dixie cup.

The heat of the afternoon lulled them to silence for a while. Finally Lomax felt her arms get heavy, and laid down her brush.

She thought she had done it with this one: the boy leaping in cobalt explosions, the scented weight of pond lilies, cattails bending over the prophets, the white woman with the devil egg in hand and the black woman under her broad straw hat, both rooted to the earth at the edge of the water. She thought she had done a good picture but refused to look at it; she could feel the image against the lids of her eyes. At any given time the completion of a picture left her dull and spent, but today she felt electrified. Distance was what she craved, and motion. She flung down her brushes and the palette as if it were the last time. Struggling to rise, she gathered the crutches under her arms.

"Where do you think you're going, young miss?" Mama asked.

"For a cruise. Down yonder by the tractor. I been meaning to inspect it. And I don't want no company either."

"Look for the tree with the branch hanging down like two snake tongues," Miss Estabelle said.

Lomax glared at the woman and then shoved off through the grass. Alphonso stood as Lomax swung forward, and she feared he would try to accompany her; but instead of following, he sang "I Surrender All" at the top of his lungs.

By the time he finished "Near to the Heart of God," Lomax was close to the rusted-out tractor that marked the end of the pasture. Every kind of vine and wildflower had overgrown the tractor shell, and countless cattle had left deposits in regard to their passing, giving the effect of a swell of ground around the flaked, corroded wheels. The effect was as if the earth were rising up to swallow the decayed metal husk. When she turned to look at the cow pond and the picnic, the blanket dwindled to the size of a postage stamp and Mama appeared no bigger than a safety pin. Miss Estabelle sat like a spider, rubbing her front legs together. Alphonso twisted, turned, leapt, chasing a dragonfly across the meadow.

Lomax swung through the grass, the soft, sharp tips tickling her legs. When she reached the tractor she guided herself round it slowly. She memorized the colors, browns and oranges, varying greens, and occasional pastels. Her arms grew tired and she wanted to sit. Out here by the tractor was no shade, but a little further, at the edge of the pine woods, she could sit on a nice cool bed of pine needles.

By the time she reached the shady woods she needed to catch

her breath and rested for a moment, looking around to find a comfortable spot. The picnic and cow pond had diminished even smaller. Silent woods and pasture surrounded her. As she moved forward on her crutches, she arced through the undergrowth with conscious quiet, as if her passage might disturb the somber day.

Out of the corner of her eye she spied something reaching down from the lower branches, seeming to move toward her, and she drew in a quick breath.

Two branches forked down from the lower limbs of a tree, smooth and curved, like snakes.

In the roots of this same tree, a bed of dry leaves, pine needles, and moss had formed, inviting her quietly.

She eased herself into the natural seat and studied the snake-branches, envisioning them as living, twisting serpents, this same shade of gray but oily and slick-looking, wrapping themselves round Miss Estabelle's arms. Lomax could hardly get her breath.

She had not realized she had come such a long way. When she settled down against the tree she recommenced her study of the rusted tractor, meaning to add it to her canvas. Now that she was here, she wished she could have brought canvas and paint with her, or that she could silently summon Alphonso to bring them. The rusted hulk seemed farther away than it should, colored like a piece of autumn, every brown shade of rot and decay. In the foreground, green flies buzzed around fresh cow pies, wildflowers, and mushrooms growing abundantly in the ordure.

She heard something nearby, small feet treading on pine needles. When she turned to see what animal it was, the sound stopped. Lomax sat perfectly still. An image passed through her head, unexplained: bare feet treading across a bed of red flowers, the feet bruising the petals as rich scent rose.

A child emerged from behind a tree, a dirty little urchin in a T-shirt.

At first she thought it was the youngest son of the Mexican woman, a boy of about this age, and she called out to him, thinking the poor toddler had strayed into the woods. But the Mexican children were shy and hesitant. The smile that lit this young boy's face knew no fear, and his dark eyes shone like chips of earth.

He smelled like flowers. A warm breeze blew from behind him, and she closed her eyes, drinking in the warmth and scent. When she opened her eyes again, the boy had stepped closer to her, and she was startled.

The child spoke some language she did not know. "I can't understand you," she said. He smiled and pointed to the trees behind him.

A cow waited there, dappled in a fall of sunlight through upper branches. The cow swished her tail in a lazy, graceless way, chewing with a look of bland contentment. The little boy spoke again, and then began to sing in a large, clear voice. The cow heard him and her ears perked up. The boy went on singing and the cow, transfixed, trotted toward him.

The child ran to meet the cow, laughing, looking back at Lomax with eyes full of delight. When he reached the cow he gripped the curled fur of its forehead and then leapt onto its generous back. Sitting there, swaying from side to side, he gazed at Lomax, his expression gradually changing. The boy wrapped his legs tight against the cow, which allowed the weight on its back without a sign of resentment. The boy studied Lomax, and finally shook his head.

Lomax dug the crutches firmly into the soft earth and struggled to her feet. "Child," she called, "come back here."

The boy blinked. He looked down at the cow, leaning to kiss her between the ears.

Lomax swung forward on her crutches. The child nudged the cow with his heels and the placid beast gradually ambled off toward the distant trees. Lomax tried to follow but couldn't keep up. The child and the cow drew farther and farther ahead of her, till finally she called out, breathless, "If you want me to follow, why won't you wait for me?"

The boy looked back at her sadly, his dark curls shining, visible till he was a long way off. Even afterward Lomax could hear him singing.

How long she stood still she could not have said. But when she turned, careful to place the crutches on firm ground, only then did she hear the commotion, the cacophony of the lowing herd that rushed toward her, feverish to reach the place into which the cow and the boy had vanished.

For a moment she was afraid. Here were the cows, as she had always expected. The whole nation of them had breached the fence and poured through, rolling toward her like a wave of water, already surrounding her. Beyond, in the meadow, her mother and Alphonso were running toward her frantically, beyond the wrecked tractor. She watched their approach with calm. Erect as a pine stood Miss Estabelle, weight on the crooked cane, her shadow tumbled over the distant picnic.

No one would reach her before the cows. She stood on the crutches feeling helpless and foolish, that she should be ending up like one of the creatures in her paintings, hopelessly trampled under the bovine of everything and laughing about it; but, finally, she turned. Heedless of her mother's voice screaming for the cows to stop right there, heedless of Alphonso, who might almost have flown across their backs to rescue her, she spun round on the crutches as the first of the sad-eyed mammals nudged her thighs with a velvet muzzle. The cows hardly seemed to be hurrying. She let them carry her forward and she kept up with their progress for a long time before they carried her downward as well, weighted and rendering her into the earth, her last silent singing of color and grace.

WALK
THROUGH BIRDLAND

HOW the dead can love you. *Stop.* How the dead can love you when you. *Stop talking.* Why they take you into the yard when they do. *Stop. Listen.* The neighbor is always listening, walking past the house without any real reason. We are among the living and the, all the living and the. Other ones. And. When they want to, when they rise up, how they can love you, forever.

You have had bad news. *You will stop talking, shut your mouth. You will lie down in the field and your heart will gather up in one knot. Flatten your palm against your mouth and bite the skin enough to feel your teeth. Your heart will gather. Shut your mouth up in one knot. Never open anything else. Die down in the field. Hard as a bone you will be one knot.*

But today we will walk through the world, into the shadowed space between the house and the abandoned yard. Lately we have been smelling the dead in the yard next door, the ones they found and the ones they didn't. The smell lingers, incredible pulsation, as if the rotting is a kind of life. As if the smell of decay has become an emanation of waves over the grass where the dead were found. Abandoned, in the yard next door, along the yard next door, you and I, we are walking . . . Then

From above they are

Showering down they are

Showering down onto the yard they are falling out of the sky they are raining through the bare branches onto the leaves onto the ground where there they are, all the grackles in the world, all the glossy grackles with blue-black heads diving and showering down through the air in the late. Searching for pecans among the unraked leaves, the birds are chattering and chiding one another, talking about that last hop, whether they are headed in the right direction, shoving and digging their beaks into the leafy humus, searching. For food is everything this time of year. Their hearts are beating furiously and yet the flock seems relaxed. The grackles take everything in stride, lifting in waves as you pass, as I pass, the one of us. We are walking through the birds, through the midst of them, and they are accepting of us, and we are one, and everything is at peace within us. We are even inside the birds and they are inside us and everything is at peace. It is a walk through birdland and we stop.

In the yard. Where they are crawling over

My feet. The birds are crawling over my feet now. But farther ahead in the yard

Then down the street he is. He is always walking past the house without any real reason. When he walks to town he never brings anything back. And the birds are crawling over my feet and they are in the high grass ahead of me in the abandoned yard and of course you will not look, you refuse, you always leave the hard part of looking to me.

Where the birds are crawling over the dead. Who can love you. Even so. With the grackles crawling over your face. The blue-black-headed birds, all of them, the world's whole population of them, crawling over your face, and you are dead, and they are not above eating you. Already, the eyes and face have suffered battery. It is no wonder you do not sit up, you dead one. It is no wonder you hide your face beneath the mask of feathers.

The neighbor passes and he sees you looking and you say, we say, we two as one, "Here's another dead one. Look."

"Yes, there's another one," the neighbor agrees.

"This one's good and dead."

"Yes, this one's good and dead."

"So," I say, and you are, naturally, hiding within; you are always quailing and hiding within at times like these.

"So," I say, "what am I supposed to do about it? I'm already late for work as it is." (A whole day late. As it is.) But anyway.

"I suppose you should call whoever you call. The ones who find dead bodies." The neighbor spoke mildly but in a clipped way.

"They already went through this yard this week," I said, slipping into the past tense myself, feeling the narrative gather force around me. "With a fine-tooth comb, they said. Those ones you were talking about, I forget the name." Sighing, firmly anchored in the past now, becoming "he." Becoming fully third person, like the neighbor. He and the neighbor stood in the yard looking at the dead one in the grass. The self-integrating sight of the dead and in fact stinking-dead corpse in the grass with the hundreds of millions of birds crawling over it and through it, very nearly through it, he and the neighbor watched this image.

The neighbor sighed and said, "It's always like this."

"What did he die of?"

The neighbor sighed again. "That thing everybody dies of. Probably."

The moment became perfect, the story culminating in the walk of the neighbor away from the yard, gloriously serene, in the golden slanting bar of a sunbeam lancing through the gap of dormers across the street, the golden lance slashing onto the neighbor, illuminating him in one final resplendent burst, a halo of alabaster fire. "It's always like this," the neighbor had said.

Even then slipping, though. I am slipping back. I am not sure if the neighbor is really gone or whether he was ever really there. I know I was never "he." I am looking at the dead one who is approaching the upright position slowly. Tedious, when the limbs no longer bend, to get up off the ground like this. But this is the gift of the dead to the living, occasionally to stand upright. We are taking the hand of the dead one, which is cold, we are walking with the grackles perched on our shoulders, heads and arms, this is the real ending, there is no narrative, we are only here, where the dead can love you sometimes, forever sometimes, in birdland.

GOD BOX

THE man came in, sat down at the God box, and started to play. He put his hands inside the box and music began. Pretty music. Nice music. Nothing else happened.

The woman came in and sat down beside him. She pursed her lips. Not only would she be forced to share the box, she would also have to begin after him. She began to play the box with a furious tightness in her fists.

"You were supposed to call me," she said. "We were supposed to come here together."

"I got tired of waiting," he said, his fingers fidgeting. She had a tone in her voice and a look on her face that caused him to cringe away from her, his body making the shape of a parenthesis. He was afraid to look at her so he looked just to the side of her.

"You should have called." After that she said nothing else and they played.

For a while the music was astounding. Coruscating over them

in waves, harmonies, and high crests, their two playings blended in the box. They closed their eyes, arched their spines and swayed, moving like the necks of what would later be called swans.

Out of the music arose a thing that grew to become the whole universe, a pulsing that sometimes died away to nothing and sometimes filled all the space around them as she and he played.

She stopped abruptly and stood and his playing faltered and the music thinned and faded. She lifted her chin and looked out the window, beyond everything else.

"I won't play with you again until you apologize," she said, and walked away, and closed the door quietly behind her.

A brief wind swept over him as he sat in front of the useless, empty box.

Around him, the music they had created gave a thorough shudder and a vast unease swept through it. Bad things began to happen everywhere.

AQUA VELVA MAN

BETWEEN exhaling and inhaling exists a moment that is hardly breathing at all. The body waits. Blood shimmers in the pleural vessels. The lungs wonder whether they will unfold again.

I had an instant like that when I saw the new attorney at the county budget meeting. I knew he could only be an attorney in that suit, standing in a posture of humility with Mr. Arly, who had trapped him in front of the doughnut table. So beautiful, his face, he could have shaved for a living, you would have watched and handed him money, gladly, for the privilege. I had heard we were getting a male attorney to replace Rhoda Goshen but I hadn't heard anything else. Now here he stood. His face, framed by steam from the coffee urn, became surreal, as if he were posing for a picture to advertise his brand of tie or watch. He signed the attendance sheet, holding the clipboard carefully, taking time to smooth the hairs on the back of his hand. The skin of his hands was a fine olive tone, very clear. All of his skin was like that, that I could see, and the flesh beneath crisp as a green apple.

He took one's breath away, to sum it up, even me and my breath, when I already worked at a hospital full of good-looking doctors. He could have been a pretty girl, he was that kind of man. *My, my,* I said to myself, and smacked my lips.

The county budget manager had prepared an agenda and her aide was passing it around. The county budget manager herself now joined Mr. Arly and the new man, and she was preening herself in front of them in spite of the fact that she was a good twenty years, maybe even thirty years, older than the new attorney. Her aide passed me with the stack of agendas and I reached for one with the hand that was partly wrapped around ledgers and printouts.

I noted the new attorney had left Mr. Arly and the county budget manager and waited very close to the seat in which I always sit at these meetings in the boardroom. My heart was pounding as I set down my two black binders, my thick green and white computer printout, and my bundle of pens, pencils, markers, compass, and six-inch ruler, all wrapped tight in a rubber band. I arranged the objects carefully with the black binders flanking my arms like wings. Someone was trying to speak to me to my right but I could only feel the radiance of the attorney, who was now choosing his own seat.

I stood and found him watching me.

"Are you the woman we're waiting for?" he asked.

It takes a certain kind of man to look dangerous in a suit. A particular shape of eye, or at least of brow, is required. He had those shapes, those angles, that made his face seem dangerous, that made his stance in the suit seem more liquid, more graceful, like an assassin, like someone who should be standing at the head of a corporate board table moving tides of fortunes. I answered something innocuous, that I was late because I had so much to carry to the meeting and could not find my cart at the last minute, my secretary had let someone borrow my cart. I realized I was speaking complete nonsense and that he was not even listening.

The other person who was trying to speak to me was the head of nursing, and she pushed her face forward into my field of vision at that very moment to ask me why I had not returned her five phone calls of this morning.

"I was getting ready for this meeting," I answered, only glancing at her mild eyes and wrinkled face.

Mr. Arly called the meeting to order then, and the man with the face, who was about to be introduced as Sterling Spector, a new partner at Farthing & Forthwright, slid into the leather chair next to mine.

In these meetings one is sometimes elevated beyond oneself. One moves from point to point on an agenda as from step to step in a dance, and all is harmony, if not accord. The county budget manager's hospital specialist was concerned that we could not document our reasons for the workload numbers we had submitted, but I was able to lead her through our thinking point by point. Mr. Arly and the county budget manager sat back in their chairs and eyed one another for reactions. Sterling Spector, impeccable and immaculate, offered a reminder concerning the contractual obligations involved, and was countered in this by the venerable Radford Orphinger of the county legal department. Our interchange took an almost organic form, with my voice and the county staff person's joined in one river of music, occasionally provided with counter-point by the reasonable-but-vaguely-adversarial tones of the attor-neys.

I had the numbers when they were needed, as I always do. We were discussing the hospital's projected workload and revenue fig-ures for the coming budget year, and I once again explained a number of interesting details concerning workload increases, par-ticularly those in the ambulatory care clinics. Workload means rev-enue if your costs are under control, as I have always said, and Mr. Arly agrees with me. But I was distracted, during this session, by the presence of Sterling Spector's elbow lying so close to my own.

When he spoke, I found myself drawn to the musical timbre of his voice. His introduction of himself to those at the meeting was, in its way, a superb performance. Mr. Arly asked him a question about the contract, and he answered, not pleading ignorance of the issues involved as any other new attorney might have done, but re-plying in the most dignified and masculine tones. He had studied the contract that required the county government to fund our pub-lic hospital operation. The particulars were very clear to him and he quoted them with complete accuracy. His voice, lighter than I had imagined it would be, sent strange pulses of heat down my spine.

A golden wedding ring glittered on his hand.

As for myself, I wore no jewelry of any kind, except for a small avant-garde-ish ceramic art brooch on the lapel of my jacket.

At the end of the meeting, when we had reached agreement on the essential numbers that would be used to advance the budget preparations, I was assigned to write a memo that summed up the meeting and to distribute the memo to all participants. Sterling Spector turned to me as the meeting began to break up and asked if he could review the memorandum prior to distribution, to make certain the legal issues were addressed.

There was something about the presumed intimacy of his tone. The way he leveled his eyes at me. It was as if he were not discussing a memo at all; I was embarrassed to look him in the eye. He had not moved his elbow from the arm of the chair. He was waiting.

There exists a brown that is golden and his eyes were full of that color. He had sandy hair combed precisely like the hair of models in men's fashion magazines, which I do occasionally buy, precisely for the worship of those faces in the pictures, those bodies in the clothes. Furthermore, he had a sharpness at the center of his eye. Why, I wondered, noting this diamond-pointed glint, why does a bit of blade entice me so? Why is a little arrogance so attractive in a man, and a lot of arrogance even more so? Why, at least, to me?

I remembered, suddenly, from earlier that morning, my cat lunging over the edge of the fountain in my backyard. I was watching from the window where I sip my morning coffee. The cat lunging, and the sudden rush of wings as my cat hooked a blue jay firmly with both paws and took it down, below the lip of the fountain, out of sight. The rush of wings, and adrenaline poured through me as I realized what I had just seen. The fountain sits in the shade of a pecan tree, and suddenly all the squirrels on the branches and all the blue jays flying between the branches set up a commotion of noise and chattering, blue jays diving toward the scene of the crime. The fountain, in its bed of hostas and a rock circle, remained motionless save for ominous, occasional stirrings of the hosta leaves.

Once I glimpsed my cat arced over the blue jay in the shadow, the cat's gaze fixed on the dying. The glint in a killer's eye is a point of light so sharp you can see it from a distance. I could see it in my cat's eyes across the yard a little after dawn. I could see it in Sterling Spector's golden irises in the boardroom of the hospital.

Farthing & Forthwright is one of the more powerful of the law firms in Atlanta, where I live. Sterling Spector's arrival in this firm and in our boardroom was itself the result of the act of a carnivore. He replaced a wonderful attorney whom I deeply respected who was, alas, a woman. Rhoda Goshen had attended hospital meetings dressed in richly colored designer dresses and draped with furs, and she perched Italian sunglasses atop her gorgeous, dark, thick hair, and sported a diamond the size of a cocktail glass on her finger. She was a woman, in short, who did not pretend to be a man in meetings, who walked about like a painting of herself, always posed, and with a brain like a minor sun. Mr. Arly did not cotton to women as his attorneys although, as in my case, we might make pretty good accountants; this was not an opinion he expressed, but it was an opinion one could watch creeping into his expression whenever he saw Rhoda Goshen. So he spoke to the senior partners at Farthing & Forthwright and Rhoda, who had spent ten years at our hospital, building her career as the brightest assistant to those very same senior partners, found herself suddenly replaced at all our meetings by Sterling Spector.

Because I was Rhoda's friend, I expected to hate Spector, until

I heard from someone who had already met him that he looked like a movie star and had the shoulders of a lumberjack.

I am sadly prone to infatuation merely on sight of a man with good shoulders and a clean-lined face. I am a sucker for a strong image. But we are not talking the crudity of, say, a bodybuilder; we are contemplating something more refined. I buy the best, most exquisite men's fashion magazines. I like the Marlboro ads even if none of those rugged faces are really cowboys. I believe in the Aqua Velva man, that strong palm splashing aftershave on that lean jaw, the glimpse of well-developed trapezius muscles on each side of his back.

But I only like to look, not touch.

So at the end of the meeting when we pushed back our chairs and the ravishing Spector turned toward me with that slight look of a predator, I experienced a flush of emotion that was as much anger as desire.

I am not one to slam notebooks on top of one another under any circumstances, even in a moment of feeling. The fact that he was watching me and that this affected my breathing in no way caused me even the slightest concern. I have a routine for leaving a meeting: I pack my papers in a certain order and make sure I carry away everything I brought. I am not one of those people who will call your secretary an hour after a meeting has ended to ask whether I left thus and such. I have never left thus and such. I have brought it back to my office with me.

"You're pretending I'm not here," he said, so softly, the voice easing up so that it barely glides into the ear.

Something touched me low in the back and I started, glancing at his hands, which were nowhere near my back. A tingle touched me. A tingling of nerves started low in the back and crept up my spine at the sound of his voice.

He was a master of this. He had exactly the right tone of voice for this. He posed with his eyes lowered slightly, an effect only I could see. To others, we seemed to be exchanging the quietest pleasantries at the end of the meeting, two neighbors in the boardroom. To me, it was clear that he understood himself only too well.

"Are you married?" he asked.

I blushed, I guess. I usually do. I would be the one who gave it away—that was a foregone conclusion.

"I'm sorry. Shouldn't I ask?"

"No. It's fine. I'm not married."

He was watching. I bent to lift the stack of papers from the table, willing that my posture should exclude him. But he said, "Let me help you with that."

"That's all right, I manage."

But he had moved past me so smoothly, with a scent of something so delicious flying up into my nostrils off the back of his neck. He had moved past me and held all my things, and his own, easily. Smiling at me, not in a friendly way, but with all the cunning of himself.

"It's a long way," I said.

"That's fine."

So I headed out the side door, as I always do, and Sterling Spector followed, past Mr. Arly, who surely noted the flush in my cheeks and the fact that Spector's arms were loaded with my belongings.

It was not a long way at all, of course, but right around the cor-

ner down the hall, and everyone saw us walking, including my secretary, Lacey Alice Long. She took one look at Sterling Spector and
reared back in her chair, nearer a swoon than I have ever seen from
anybody. Handsome men have that effect on Lacey; it is something
she and I have in common, even though she is three years from her
retirement and I am thirty-three years from mine.

"Where do you want these?"

"You can set those right here on my desk," Lacey Alice answered, smacking her palm on the blotter that covered the center.
"All that stuff is really mine."

"Is it?"

"Oh yes. I do all the work around here. Except for the meetings, Miss Hopper just sets back with her feet on her desk." Lacey
Alice laughed and all her chins throbbed. "That's a joke."

Sterling laughed, a mild sound. He turned to me. "I'd really
like to talk to you in your office for a moment."

The momentary widening of panic in my eyes must have
pleased him, since he smiled slightly. But Lacey Alice, seated below
us, understood what the panic signified.

"Now, Miss Hopper, don't you forget you have another meeting," she began.

But Sterling had already moved inside and stood as if the room
beyond were his own office.

He closed the door. That gave me time to reach the other
side of my desk. But when I turned again, the massiveness of his
good-lookingness struck me again. He smoothed the sides of his
hair as a way of composing himself, and gave the floor a calculat-
ing sweep with his eyes. "I've heard a lot about you from the

other people here at the hospital. Now, meeting you, I've become very curious."

"I was a good friend of Rhoda's."

"I know. That's one reason I followed you back to your office."

"What happened to her was a shame."

"I know that. But it has nothing to do with what happened to me."

I laughed in spite of myself, in spite of the fact that I found myself a little breathless watching the perfect leaf-spread of veins across the back of his hand. He had unbuttoned his jacket and now, when he leaned forward, the jacket fell open. One could see his lean, flat waist. I could see. There was something delicious about the tautness of the waist within the softness of the fabric. "You took Rhoda's place," I said, my own words startling me, because I could hear the distance between what I was thinking and the words themselves. "Of course it has something to do with you."

"But not with anything that I did. You see," he said, still leaning forward sincerely, setting his knuckles flat on my desk, "I need allies here, and I was hoping you would be one."

·   ●   ●

He left my office soon after. I did have another meeting in an hour, and tried to prepare for it.

That night when he called me at home, I felt oddly unsurprised. He had smelt prey. My scent, as I knew, had a degree of weakness in it, and the predator usually seeks this sign, that his weapons are functioning as they ought.

I had been pacing in the bar and kitchen of my duplex in Grant

Park, listening to the thumping on the wall I shared with my tenants, wondering what sort of damage they were doing to their half of my house. I had hidden the issues of *GQ* and *Esquire* out of sight, along with my latest fetish, an underwear catalog from California, full of images of tight-bodied young men who were probably gay; whenever I looked at these pictures I often said to myself, *These are pictures of men who are probably gay*, which I found satisfying. That somehow completed the circle. I became even more uninvolved.

I had no reason to hide the magazines now, since he could not possibly come to my house, not possibly, since Sterling did not know where I lived. My phone number is unlisted so even the enterprising cannot find it. But I piled the magazines in the bottom of the utility closet and spread over them the paint-stained sheet that I use to cover the cans of paint I keep for touch-ups.

The phone rang. I knew it would be him. It was my sister. We talked. I hardly heard a word she said, something about Kevin, her fat two-year-old. She also fretted about Mom. We agreed to worry together and then said good-bye. The phone rang. I knew it would be him. It was.

I held the phone with a heightened sense of awareness. I listened to the tone of voice more than the words, but even that much was a mistake, because the tone reached all the way down my lower back again, a river of sensation flowing the length of the spine.

He had called on the chance that I had been affected by our meeting today. His and mine. He had been affected and he hoped I had. He didn't usually make this kind of a phone call, he hoped I understood that. But sitting next to me in the meeting, he had become aware once again that very interesting people have an aura

that attends them, a way of being in space. I was one of those people. He could feel me when he was sitting beside me and he could
feel me now, through the telephone line. He could feel my special
strength. Maybe he sounded a little silly, maybe he was going overboard, but this was how he felt.

One listens to these things. One wants to hear them. Even
though one knows them to be ridiculous. Even though one sentence barely follows from the one before it.

"Why are you saying all this to me?"

"Because I think you need something from me."

           ·   •   ●

He wanted to drive to my house that night. I said I did not think
that would be a good idea. I did not say, I am under legal constraint.

Reason to panic. I panicked. I paced the floors. I drank the
other half of the beer I had put back into the refrigerator after
work. It was a lot for me, these two halves of a whole beer in one
evening. I was tipsy. I even felt the room spinning a little. He
would call again. The phone did ring again, too, and I knew it was
him, I knew he would not leave me alone. It was my mother, wanting to talk about my sister.

Instead, he knocked on the door.

It was, I reflected, what the Marlboro man would have done.

Outside I looked for wherever he might have tied up his horse.
He had parked on the street, the exact dark, rounded, European-
type sports car I would have guessed he'd have. He may have felt the
intent of my gaze, glancing backward. "I parked out there," he said.

"How did you know where I lived?"

He shrugged. "I found out. Are you going to let me come in?"

The obvious organ was pounding. I avoided looking at him too directly, but even an indirect glance was enough to tell me that he was as lovely in casual clothes as he had been in the suit. Standing aside, I let him pass, and a flood of danger filled the house.

I'm under legal constraint. He is an attorney.

He had taken off his wedding ring. I saw this when he turned.

His eyes changed. He needed something. There was that glint, the killer edge.

"I like your place."

"Thanks."

"You own this."

"And the other half, too. The place next door."

He wandered around the room a little. I understood he was waiting for me to do something, maybe to tell him to sit down, maybe to come closer to him. Something.

I thought, I will tell him and he will laugh softly. He will think it is all a joke at first, or else he will not think anything, he will simply hear my words, and wait. I will tell him and he will stand there for a minute. Then his face will change, the look of the hunter will leave his eyes. He will become more guarded, suddenly. He will sit without asking. I will tell him my news, then the reason that he drove to my house, that he learned my address and found me here, will not seem so apparent to him anymore, and he will not look at me anymore like I am something that he is chasing down, a rabbit that has broken for cover in front of his hound.

"Does it make you angry that I came?"

"No."

"I'm the kind of man who usually goes after what he wants. Like finding out your address."

He was giving me a long, intense look. I will tell him now, in the middle of this look. But for some reason I was crossing the room, I was coming closer to him, being led by the low of the back, as if his hand were there.

Up close he was as beautiful as any angel, any portrait of anybody, anywhere in the world. Skin so clear you thought your finger would pass right through it. He was watching me with that hint of arrogance that he must have carefully cultivated. His mouth was opening. I expected the edges of his teeth to glint. His real hand was now circling my waist, his real touch at the base of my spine.

I believe in the image of man. I believe in the goodness of the image, the clean jawline, the curled lip. There is little that motion can add to such an image.

I told him. I said the words I am required to say by law in Georgia. Or also, that I am required by myself to say. I wondered, *Why am I saying this so fast? Why can't I find a way to keep the message back a while?*

But I told him. He sat without asking. His face shifted.

"That changes things, I guess," I said.

He sat with his jaw in his hand, looking at the floor.

"You know, it's a law in this state, I have to tell you."

He glared at me, his face full of pure hate. I had never seen such a sudden shift and for a moment I could not breathe, my lungs refused to move. The next moment he got himself under control, the veins at his temples pounding. Sweat broke out across his brow. All this happened very quickly, and he never said a word.

He pulled himself up from my chair, lurching heavily, as if his weight had suddenly increased. He stood there for a moment bewildered, then made his way to the door.

"If you tell anybody about this, I'll sue you," I said.

When he was gone I stood there. I could hardly believe what I had done, that the words had passed my lips at all. I wondered why it had been so easy, really, to tell Sterling Spector this news that would send him away.

In the closet I threw off the painted sheet and stood over the stacks of magazines. I believe in them all, in all the beautiful faces, in all the perfect bodies, I believe in the beauty of these shapes and forms. Here is the goodness of these things, on these pages. Captured like the scent in perfume, I believe.

But I could not leave the magazines uncovered like that, and I could not bring myself to move them back into the house. So I spread the sheet carefully, and closed the door.

WE MOVE
IN A RIGOROUS LINE

HE sat in an airplane heading helplessly out to sea. He had a wonderful view of the night, the clear stars glittering above him and
the water shifting and sparkling far below. All his life he had loved
clear, calm nights like this one. In the vastness the plane hardly
seemed to move at all, suspended between gulfs of ocean and sky.
He was able to smile as he counted the constellations, it was easy in
such a quiet, even now, to be calm.

At the console the pilot slumped over his senseless instruments.
Mr Winchester felt sorry for the pilot, who had been very nice as
pilots go, helping Mr Winchester to his seat on the plane with a
careful sense of Mr Winchester's dignity, lifting Mr Winchester out
of the wheelchair as if he lifted all his passengers out of wheelchairs
and carried them to their seats like sacks of fertilizer. He talked the
whole time, telling joke after joke till finally even Mr Winchester
had to laugh. Though often he did not appreciate the best jokes.
The pilot folded the wheelchair and stowed it somewhere at the

back of the jet. The aide who had driven Mr Winchester to the air-
field waited politely till the pilot fastened the hatch. A serene dark-
ening evening. "We should have a good flight," the pilot said.

Takeoff went smoothly, but soon they flew into a storm. Still
the pilot took pains to soothe Mr Winchester, cracking jokes about
the winds that shook the plane and the lightning they could see
flashing for miles on either side. The rain beat heavy on the cockpit glass. The pilot said they would just have to fly over this here
little storm and radioed for permission to cruise at a higher altitude. The quiet voice of an air controller from Memphis informed
the pilot he might take the plane to twenty-five thousand feet and
the pilot began to do so cleanly and gracefully. Mr Winchester relaxed against the seat and tried to read a legal paper from his briefcase. When they headed into the cloud layer things got bumpy
again, and the pilot laughed and tried to think of something to say.
Calming an old man's nerves, Mr Winchester thought, but then the
pilot leaned forward, anxiously scanning one of those dials of his,
and after that he made no more jokes. Air became thin. The pilot
tapped a gauge with an anxious fingertip. He turned around to Mr
Winchester and opened a compartment over his head. A plastic
mask tumbled down and the pilot said, "This is just for safety."

He put the mask over Mr Winchester's nose and mouth, humming a shrill tune. The mask was cold, and the air it guaranteed him
had a sweet smell. "Is something wrong?" Mr Winchester asked.

"We're losing pressure. I think we are, anyway; my gauge is
fouled." He patted the knee that Mr Winchester could not feel.
"We may have to land in Birmingham but we'll be all right."

He turned around and reached for the compartment over his

own head. But the plane bumped suddenly and an air hose began
to hiss. The pilot had got hold of the compartment latch but now
he seemed to forget what to do with it. His fingers opened and
closed. He looked sleepy and nodded his head. The plane bucked
again as if a large hand had given it the merest shake, and the cabin
lights went out. The pilot relaxed in his seat as if he didn't have any
idea where he was. Mr Winchester called out to him and the pilot
nodded his head once. But he closed his eyes in the same motion
and began to bleed from his nose and from the corner of his
mouth. After that Mr Winchester didn't call him any more. From
the console sounded the whirring of the autopilot and from every
side the rain drummed against the helpless machine.

Over the radio came the voice from Memphis asking that the pilot conform his altitude. Mr Winchester leaned forward as far as he
could and watched the lighted instruments register their simple numbers for the benefit of nobody. He thought the biggest dial was the al-
timeter but the pale numbers blurred and ran together. He pressed the
oxygen mask against his face now that he knew how precious it was.
The air hose was long enough that he could move a little in the seat.
He shifted his weight with his hands, watching the pilot's wheel turn
silently back and forth. The needles in the gauges flickered like candle
flames. Wisps of cloud flung themselves at the cockpit glass, where Mr
Winchester could see the watery reflection of his own face peering
calmly out, swallowing the clouds with a slight smile and bleary eyes.
He had peered calmly out in just this way at a hundred board meetings, had turned the same bleary eyes on a thousand precisely-typed
legal documents, but this was new. The voice of the Memphis air controller asked for confirmation of the plane's altitude as twenty-one

thousand feet. The voice called again, sounding infinitely distant, asking for response in that professional voice that showed no sign of concern. Now the pilot seemed to be laughing. The plane climbed higher and higher with hardly a whisper, though Mr Winchester could hear the muffled rush of the wind.

After a while the plane broke free of the clouds. Thousands of stars appeared, more than he had seen at one time in years, and suddenly he remembered walking an open field at night when he was a boy, seeing these same fierce masses of stars burning endlessly in the black sky. When he was a boy he had dreamed of flying. Now the sight of the stars brought to him a sense of both ends of his life, and beyond his life, and for a long time he sat watching them. No voice called for any confirmation over the radio. The air from the mask tasted sweet. The plane flew in a straight line over the clouds, and Mr Winchester pictured the curve of the climb as a bow with a span of a thousand miles. He pictured the plane as if he floated far from it watching its flight: slim and white, moving senselessly and beautifully forward through the clear air, its quiet jets pouring out streams of gases. All storms abandoned far below. Soon there were no more clouds to be seen, only the gulf below and above, the little jet suspended between two enormities. He almost smiled at the thought that he would end up moving at so many hundreds of miles an hour when for years he hadn't walked a single step under his own strength. He flew over mountains with starlight shimmering on the peaks, he flew over cities stretched like constellations over the black surface of earth. Now and then he could see traffic lights change colors at miniscule intersections. He had no idea what part of the world he was looking at any more, though he guessed he might still be headed vaguely for Virginia. Maybe he would fly right over the Charlottesville airstrip where his lawyers were waiting for him. He was buying a horse farm in Albemarle County. Once he had been an avid rider of horses, and was still fond of watching them run. Nowadays his nieces rode the horses and he sat with a blanket over his lap in the shade of walnut trees, looking out over meadows that rolled like green clouds. He had meant to retire to the horse farm, and sit there for the rest of his life.

From the radio a broken voice announced that he had entered the eastern air defense zone and was required to identify himself. When the voice repeated the demand he answered, "I am Thomas Bell Winchester, principal shareholder and president of Thomas Bell Winchester Industries, worth several million dollars and very tired." The voice warned him that air force intercepters were on the runway ready to pursue should he continue to refuse response. The voice announced his altitude as thirty-five thousand feet and climbing, bearing northeast over Gettysburg, headed toward the seacoast in a straight line. A new voice joined the first, demanding that the unidentified aircraft break radio silence, and then another voice confirmed radar contact with the intruder. He guessed these would be the pilots of the air force interceptors, but he did not see either jet pass over the plane that carried him so silently. He heard them both report what they saw and noted the puzzlement in their voices. When they passed close to him to read the registration on his plane, he glimpsed the mask one of the pilots wore, much more elaborate than his own. At the sight of the military jet he withdrew from the window. "There's nobody flying that thing," the pilot said. In a halting voice the other pilot confirmed the registration for the air controller in Norfolk, and added, "I don't see anybody either. This is spooky."

He wondered if they would check the plane's numbers in time for him to hear them say his name just once. The three planes flew silently on and on. He tried to look past them to the stars. He took deep breaths of oxygen and felt calm again. Distantly he told himself he had things to do and ought to get these air force planes to help him save his life; he had vague visions of himself struggling over these seats, taking hold of that idiotic wheel and landing the jet at some lonely beachside airstrip; but he had relaxed at last, it seemed. The plane moved forward with its own will, following that sere simple line, and he gave way to it completely. When one of the pilots read his altitude as forty thousand feet and climbing he laughed into the mask.

Now they were flying over the ocean. One of the pilots asked if anyone knew how many people were supposed to be on board that thing and the air controller read from the dispatch terminal that the plane belonged to a private company called the Eastern Exploration Group, and that there were only two people on board, the pilot Mong McHenry and some rich bigwig from an oil company. He listened for his name but the controller never said it. He watched the glittering water and the cold sky. He closed his eyes and felt his heart pounding like horses' hooves on meadow grass. The plane's engine jerked and shuddered.

The largeness of the world he had always lived in awed him at the last. The engines shivered, eating shreds of fuel, and his palms grew moist on the seat arms. Yes, this was everything. The engines shuddered again. He tried to picture how it looked from a distance, when the tiny plane stalled in its silly climb, took a sweeping curve and submitted to gravity. He could feel it in his stomach. For a moment the water was the sky and then it was everything, a shimmering that rose toward the cockpit like an endless hand. He pictured his plummeting through miles of air and let the descent relax him as if it would last forever. He had a vision of a city in the water where the streets were clean and the houses new, and he was walking along a street toward a temple or a high-rise office building, only he had no briefcase to carry, his hands were free and empty. Last of all, before the water took him, he heard the Norfolk air controller make an odd high sound, the note of a song he had heard somewhere, maybe long ago, falling off into nothingness and endless void.

JESUS IS SENDING YOU THIS MESSAGE

NO telling how many times I had ridden home beside her on the train before she gave the message and I noticed. Sitting sleek and composed, with her hands clamped firmly on her purse, she was, that day, dressed primly in a pleated skirt and sensible shoes of navy blue, with a bright, fluffy scarf tied at her throat. An older woman, of the generation in which proper ladies wore gloves, like those she carried, folded in her hands, she was blessed with smooth, supple skin the color of dark roast coffee beans; it would have been a flawless skin except for the tiny moles growing out of some of her pores. Her nose was broad and rounded at the end. Her silver-blue hair, streaked, straightened, and shaped into sweeping curves, encased her skull like a helmet, and when she moved the whole stiff mass moved with her, protecting the delicate workings inside, the receiver into which Jesus beamed the message.

She wore a hat that first day I heard her speak, of navy blue felt, with a round brim nicely upturned, and a satin ribbon around

the crown, resting gently on the waves and spikes of her hairdo.
She rocked forward in her seat, hands clasped around her purse,
and glanced at everyone around her. Her eyes brushed mine with
the slightest hesitation and moved on. Moments later, she said, in
a loud, firm voice, "Good evening, everybody. How is everybody
doing?"

She waited, with a fresh, open look, perfectly unafraid. I felt a
moment of discomfort, standing so close to her, thinking she was
just another crazy person talking on the train while the rest of us
made our way home from a day's work in downtown Atlanta. Quiet
grew around her and she allowed it to reach its maximum radius,
then continued. "Jesus told me to give this message to the people.
The Lord is coming back soon, the wait is nearly over. You need to
be getting right with God, you don't have much time. Woeful days
are coming, when he will bring a destruction on all wickedness of
all peoples. Fire will burn in the cities and hellfire and damnation
will come to them that have earned it. Then Jesus will come like
the light of all things, amen. So you need to hear the message this
time, because the Bible says it will come—a destruction on the
cities, even on this city, too, and it will be too late for you once Jesus gets here. That's what Jesus told me to tell the people. Thanks
for listening."

Sitting back with a sense of gliding, at the end she gave a nervous look in various directions, including a glance into my face, the
only glimmer of fear she showed, or so I fancied; and she showed
that same moment of fear and hesitation every time I saw her, or
else I imagined it each time.

The moment passed and I was left with a vague irritation, that first day, but nothing more. But the next morning I boarded the train and found her waiting again, in the exact seat but this time wearing one of those cotton dresses made of hunter-green fabric covered with white polka dots, a white collar, big white buttons down the front, a white belt and a full skirt. Her bosom swelled ample and high over the cinched belt. A white hat rode the whorls of her hair. She had the same look on her face, as if an invisible page hung before her eyes, words only she could see. Moments after the train left King Memorial Station, she shifted forward, rolling on those ample hips, and glanced at me and opened her mouth and spoke.

I felt, then and later, that she aimed her message at me, though this must have been my imagination, since outwardly she gave no sign of noticing me in any particular way, other than to glance at me with all the rest. But even as early as that second hearing she made me angry with this message, spoken that time so early in the morning. The train arrived at the Georgia State Station and I burst out the door, hurtling toward the escalator. On the short, humid walk to my job at a nearby hospital, I seethed with thoughts of the message giver which only subsided when I reached my office and found the classical music station playing Bach's Goldberg Variations, soothing piano by Konstantin Lifschitz, enabling me to breathe again.

She became a fixture in my life, after that. She gave the message mornings and afternoons, though most often in the afternoons, always from a seated position, always on the tracks between the Georgia State Station and the Martin Luther King Jr. Memorial Station. I heard her give the speech going in both directions, and the message never varied, even by one word. She had clearly rehearsed these sentences, and the thought of this added to my resentment of her. She spoke calmly, not with the fervor of a prophet but rather with the grace of a Sunday school teacher. Completing the message as the train pulled into one station or the other, she composed herself and settled back against her seat. By the time the doors opened and new passengers boarded, no one would ever have known that she had, only moments before, shared with us her certainties about the end of time.

Each day, each instance of the message, filled me with contempt for this need she had to put herself forward, to flaunt her Christianity in that manner. Each moment when she shifted forward in her seat to commence her little sermon, I glared at her with narrowed eyes as if I could silence her with the completeness of my disapproval.

I am an educated man, a cultivated man. I am not the type of person who would ever speak aloud on a train, unless there were some purpose to it, as, saying to the person next to me, "Excuse me, you are standing on my foot," or, "Please take your elbow out of my lungs." I am the type of person who believes other people should obey the same rules I do, among them, namely, that no one should presume to deliver Golgothan messages on a commuter train when people are tired and simply want to get home as peaceably as possible. It seemed clear to me that this message could not come from Jesus because He would be too polite to send it. So I listened to her words every day, during a period of peak ridership, in transit from Georgia State to King Memorial or vice versa; and I disliked her every day as well, increasingly.

I see that I have claimed this happened every day. But when I examine my memories, I understand that, while frequently we did ride in the same car on the same train, just as frequently we did not. In the afternoon, I most often caught the 4:36 p.m. eastbound on my way home. Being a creature who takes comfort in habits, I always entered the Georgia State Station from the same direction, crossed the vaulted lobby at the same angle, climbed the same four flights of granite steps to the platform and waited there next to the same wooden bench. Never sitting on the bench, for fear of dirtying my trousers. But I waited precisely in that spot for the train, because I had calculated from experience that most of the time the lead car pulled up to that point and I had only to step forward to be aboard.

In the mornings I followed a similarly exact routine riding from Inman Park to King Memorial and then on to Georgia State.

On some afternoons I reached the platform only to find the train waiting, and in that case I stepped into the nearest door; or I reached the platform as the door chimes rang and the doors slid closed in my face and then I had to wait for the 4:43 p.m. train; or someone was standing in my waiting place and I had to wait somewhere else and board the wrong car; or someone from work offered me a ride; or I was sick or on vacation or holiday; on many days I never saw her, never heard her give the message. But most afternoons my precise timing and luck brought me to the same place, to the space in the alcove, studying the faded roses on the message woman's cloth bag.

She was a creature of habit like me and liked to sit in one of those seats next to my support pole, or the ones across from me and my pole, so that she was always riding sideways on the train. When I had heard the message often enough to expect her, even to presume she would be sitting there, I began to dread her as well, as soon as I climbed to my waiting place on the platform; though I refused to vary my own routine. I listened for the sounds of the approaching train, watched for the splash of light along the tunnel wall. By the time the train pulled to a stop in front of me and I stepped forward to be the first in line, to board the train first, I had already begun to hate her, as though I knew she were there, as though I could see her sitting with that air of purpose in her usual seat. When I stepped onto the train, when I saw her sitting with that purse raised up like the defensive wall of a highly rounded city, my contempt boiled to loathing and I stood in my usual place fuming that she was certain to speak again, that she would say those words from Jesus that were so intrusive, words that should not be spoken in a public place where people are trapped and have no choice but to listen.

She did, without fail, speak that message each time I saw her. Moving forward in her seat and glancing at her audience, in spite of my longing for her silence, she spoke.

I began to feel, during her soliloquy, the impulse to answer her back, to say, Jesus did not send any message through you for me. The idea of talking back to her, once formed, became part of the whole routine. In my head I framed messages that I would like to give her, brief scenes in which I triumphed over her there on the train; in which I, in fact, transformed her, causing her to understand that there are people in this world who do not need revealed truth on commuter trains or, indeed, in any other setting, excepting perhaps that of the church. There are decent, Christian folk who do not care to live with visions of burning destruction, who are content whether Jesus should come back or not; who are, in fact, happy to wait for him as long as He chooses to tarry. In my fantasy she was overcome with shame at her own effrontery and slid, chagrined, flat against her seatback, never again uttering even a sigh.

My fantasies entirely convinced me of my own way of thinking, so that, when she slipped slightly forward in her seat and gave that sweeping glance to those standing closest, for a long time I thought my silent fury rose up because of the rudeness of her remarks, because her words were not wanted by anybody. I was a Christian myself, a churchgoer, and I did not wish to hear them.

But then one day, at the close of the message, when the woman was easing back into her seat, another black woman seated near her said, "Amen, sister," in a loud, clear voice, and an elderly white man nodded his head serenely, as if Jesus had told him the same thing; and I became more angry than ever.

The next day, trembling in my waiting place, the certainty that she would be present engendered in me a shivering rage. I heard the familiar drawn-out hoot of the train in the tunnel and witnessed its glide into the station, and I stepped across the platform in the usual way and suddenly realized the train had pulled up too far, that my special door was not where it was supposed to be, and I was actually forced to push and shove my way onto the train with the rest. The train filled to overflowing, I suppose because the train before it had been delayed, and when the doors closed I could not see whether the message woman was there or not I remained ignorant, my heart fluttering, until, a few dozen yards down the track, her familiar voice rang out, "Good evening, everybody. How is everybody doing?"

I ground my back teeth together and pursed my lips and frowned to get the hard line between my eyebrows. I am a tooth grinder, as my dentist will tell you, and I flex my jaw almost constantly, and awaken some mornings with tension headaches and the fear that I will soon have facial cancer. But at especial times I grind my teeth in anger, and I did so that afternoon on the train.

I began to study the other people. At first I detected only those who agreed with her, the other older black women, dressed as she was dressed, with what one might describe as a churchwoman's flare for the benign; and, sometimes, older, white women dressed in a similar vein who signaled their approval demurely with their eyes; or else women of a lower class who nodded, their faces elastic with expanding wrinkles, and said, "You're speaking for the Lord now," and raised their hands for a little of that invisible Holy Ghost that is always present in the air.

My only allies were, in fact, silent men and groups of teenagers, who were always guaranteed to burst into gales of laughter when she finished speaking the message. Once a loud and sassy girl with huge round thighs and buttocks waited till the end of the message and said, in a crisp, loud voice, "Old grammaw," and her friends hooted and ducked their heads slapping each other this way and that. The message woman simply blinked and watched the space on the wall directly across from her head, as if nothing penetrated the world in which she sat.

A moment later, with breathtaking grace, she leaned forward without looking down and pulled, from the cloth bag, a Bible so worn and thumbed it could only be called formidable, covered in black leather, with patches of bright gold on the edges. She opened the book and started to read silently from the New Testament, one of the gospels where all Jesus' speeches flared up from the page in red ink. The teenagers watched her and fell mostly silent, though one of them would snicker now and then.

One night I dreamed of her lips as she shaped the word "woeful," the fact that the shape of the lips scarcely resembled the sound; her need to replenish her lipstick became very clear to me. She favored a strong red, though not too much of it. Her lips were dark brown at the edges, tapering to pink on the inside. In the dream I saw all this very clearly. Then I awoke with the sheets damp at my neck and a drop of sweat on my meager chest hairs and I became terrified.

I attended St. Luke's Episcopal Church on Peachtree Street, a fine old liberal church with a respectful pastor who occasionally challenged his congregation to greater sacrifice but certainly never threatened us with fiery destruction. While our congregation offered less prestige than a Buckhead church, I felt it was the next best thing. During services, I found myself watching my neighbors on the pews, the young professionals side by side with the old professionals, the gays, the blacks, the well-dressed and the gauchely dressed, the matrons, the widowers, the boys, the girls, the children, the teenagers, the wild bunch, the quiet ones: I studied them, the mostly white faces, and wondered what touch of God would be required to get any of them to speak on a train? Or to hear a message from God at all?

I have heard of white people attending church services in black congregations, like the African Methodist Episcopal Church, or, more often, the Ebenezer Baptist Church in Sweet Auburn, the

historic district of downtown Atlanta where Martin Luther King
Sr. was a preacher and Martin Luther King Jr. became known to
the world. But now, when I rode through the shadows of those
black churches, I wondered what sort of religion could be practiced
there, to arouse in such an ordinary woman the need to predict the
end of time to perfect strangers. To speak on a train, actually to do
so, to move forward in her seat and open her mouth—how long
had she felt the need to take this action before she had delivered the
message for the first time? And the words that she spoke, where did
they come from? Did Jesus speak to her in a way He never employed with me?

Seated in the wooden pew of the St. Luke's Episcopal sanctu-
ary, listening to the swell of the organ playing one more verse of
"Just as I Am, Without One Plea," I listened for the voice of God,
even for the echo of the voice of God as He spoke to someone
else, and I heard only our thin, reedy voices risen somewhat in
song. Then it occurred to me, the question that finally drove me to
take action: Was the Christ in her church, who filled her mouth
with speech, more real than the Christ in mine?

One day she wore a gold brooch with a silver enamel center
and I stood so close to her I could see myself reflected in its surface,
a helpless, ridiculous expression on my tiny, pinched face. She had
yet to give the message that day, the train having only begun to
slide out of Georgia State Station along the curve of track beyond,
and I had been forced to stand far closer to her than ever before;
added to that, the brooch offended me deeply, being so large and
rounded, jutting out from her white rayon blouse with its fussy
ruffled collar. But even more offensive was the presence of my own

reflection in the milky surface of the brooch, nested near the center of her cleavage. Impossible that I should be so reflected, that my
image should seem so tiny and insignificant. The volcano of anger
at last boiled over as she rolled those large hips forward and smiled
and said those words of preamble, "Good evening, everybody. How
is everybody doing?"

"Everybody is doing fine without your message," I said. "Why
don't you, for once, sit there and shut your mouth."

As if she had foreseen just such a moment, she hesitated in her
forward motion and raised her eyes to mine. In the eyes I saw neither mildness nor serenity but a sharp pinpoint of fury. People
around us were tittering and whispering and pointing as the ripple
of my words spread out across our pond. "Who does he think he
is, what's wrong with him?" I heard, but she kept her eyes glued to
mine through that instant, and spoke without hesitation back to
me. "I believe I am welcome to speak Jesus' words on this train,"
she said, "and God bless you in your heart." Then, smiling again,
she leaned forward and began, as always, as if I had said nothing, as
if I were not present at all. "Good evening, everybody. How is
everybody doing? Jesus told me to give this message to the people."

Those around us listened raptly, and I stood there, unable to re-
cede. She spoke with the calm that had been absent from her eyes
when she turned her face up to mine, and she delivered the message with the same precision, even the same pauses, as on every
other occasion. Her hands she folded over her purse, her white gloves
folded in her hands, the small bit of veil from her hat arranged at-
tractively over her forehead. She spoke "Woeful times are coming"
with that movement of lips of which I had dreamed; she was in

need of a touch of lipstick, I noted, even in my distraction and mortification. I had dreamed this actual moment, I too had fore-seen everything.

She completed the message and returned to her resting posi-tion. She never so much as glanced at me. Those around her ap-proved of every word, a few "Amens" were whispered, and many faces, black and white, glared at me disapprovingly for my rudeness.

Why had I spoken? Was it simply my reflection in the awful brooch? Had my workday at the hospital piqued my temper to that point? Or was it worse than that? Had I felt so free to speak to this woman for reasons I hardly cared to imagine?

At Inman Park Station I stumbled from the open door and felt the relief of all those who remained behind me. I wondered what they said to one another after I fled. In my mind, like an endless reel of film, the whole sequence of moments replayed itself again and again: my anger, my reflection in the brooch, my sudden, un-thinking need to spit words at her, and all that followed, the whole moment of her triumph and my humiliation.

Afterward, I could no longer follow the course of my old habits. I changed everything to avoid her, taking an earlier train from Inman Park and heading home on, as a rule, the 4:50 p.m. train from Geor-gia State Station. I abandoned my old standing-and-waiting place for a location far down the platform, on the bridge that crosses over Piedmont Avenue below the State Capitol Building, where I could see the gleaming dome of real gold leaf. But, as happens, one after-noon when hurrying to the train, I found it had already arrived at the station and I darted heedlessly into the first open door. She was sitting in her usual place and saw me at once; she lifted her face and knew me, I am certain of it, but she said nothing at all. My heart pounded and I nearly fled to the other end of the car; but then I got my breath and held my ground and waited. This time I will listen, I thought. This time I will hear her message as if it really comes to me from Jesus, and I will receive these words into my heart, and I will change; I will never be angry again.

But she merely sat there and never moved forward, never spoke. Her worn Bible showed itself in the faded flowered bag but she never lifted it out, never opened it or read it. The train reached King Memorial Station and still she had not spoken, nor would she meet my eye again. She simply gazed, placid and withdrawn, at the advertisement for Bronner Brothers hair care products behind my head, and at the passing landscape through the windows—the cemetery where Margaret Mitchell was buried, the old cotton sack factory, and the chic renovated cottages of Cabbagetown. We rode to Inman Park and I left the train, feeling hollow and even bereft.

At home I bagged the garbage and walked and fed Herman, my aging schnauzer. The life of a bachelor has always suited me, I have never wanted much company, but that evening I called a friend from church and asked her out to dinner. She made some excuse, clearly embarrassed by the invitation, and I hung up the phone feeling even lonelier than before. I felt as if I had been drifting out to sea for a very long time without noticing, and that today I had lost sight of land forever, my continent disappearing over the horizon, while I drifted on and on. I felt the urge to cry and wish, now, I could report that I actually had.

I have seen the message woman since, on occasion. She rides the train as I do, every day, though where she boards and where she departs I have never learned. I picture her as a schoolteacher or teacher's aide, or as a librarian, perhaps employed in Midtown or in West End near the Joel Chandler Harris house. I picture her surrounded by children to whom she tells stories, and sometimes I try to imagine the stories she might tell, rolling words pouring out of her in that voice that had become, at one time, so very familiar to me. Most often I picture her in the front pew of a church, enraptured by the power of some thunderous sermon descending over her from the mouth of a faceless preacher, surrounding her with the voice of God.

When I am present with her, I know she recognizes me and always will, as the white man who told her to shut up, who tried to stifle Jesus' message. She sits neatly and silently folded in the seat, and I stand in my narrow space with my arms glued to my side, my breath coming a bit labored. She waits, and I wait, but no message comes. I slide out of the train at my appointed place and picture her then, moving forward in the seat as the train accelerates toward the next station up the line; she glances around at everybody and begins again, wetting her lips and speaking those words that I hear, these days, all the more clearly in her silence.

PEGGY'S PLAN

FIRST, I would reach out to those who have been tortured. There are places where many horrible tortures are practiced, and I would go there as soon as I realized my powers. For instance, in brick buildings with no windows deep in the suburbs of Washington, D.C., there are rooms with horrible torture chairs. Or in the back rooms of military ministry buildings of various nations. I would find these buildings, and, for instance, if someone had vicious metal implements shoved under the fingernails, I would draw out the implements, and I would run my fingers over the bloodied mess, and the hands would heal, and there would be no more pain. I could even erase the memory of pain from the tortured one, although this might be presumptuous.

It might take a while to reach all those who have been maimed and vivisected in the name of this or that. I would have to move in hidden ways for a while and heal all the tortured before moving on to the political arena. For instance, in the case of truly horrible tortures, like amputations or tongue-rippings or ghastly events involving the nipples, it might take me some time to heal the damage, since I am only one miracle worker. It could require some effort for me to grow back a leg on somebody who has had one cut off in an arbitrary way. This part of the healing of the tortured I will have to play by ear. But I would expect that I could pretty much solve the problem of torture within about six months to a year.

Then afterward it would be a choice between healing the sick and afflicted and the perfecting of all human governments. I have had to do a lot of thinking about this, Sister, and I do think it is important to get rid of all diseases as soon as possible. I am sure it is more important to get rid of the diseases before the poverty, for instance, but I am having trouble deciding whether it would be better to tackle the diseases right after the tortured people, or whether it would be better to go ahead and perfect the governments first. This is a matter of prioritizing.

So we will think about this for a moment. I believe it will take a lot of time to heal all of the sick, especially the ones sick with diseases that are yet unknown and unrecognized. There will be a lot of convincing of people and backing and forthing and so on. I will say you are sick, for instance, and that I need to heal you, and you will say you feel perfectly all right. Then I will say, yes, you are sick, because I know, and I will tell you what kind of disease you have and if you have not heard of this disease you will look at me like I am a loony. This will put up a block but I will heal you anyway; it will just take more time. When you think about how many sick people there are and you add up all the extra time, it is for sure that the problem of the sick will take some investment.

It is possible that I could just abolish all sickness at one time, with one gesture, so to speak. Like, I wave my hand and there is no more sickness of any kind. But in reality it seems to me, Margaret Ann Hammacker, that everybody will want their own individual healing and that even if I did wave my hand and abolish disease, a lot of people wouldn't believe that it was gone until I healed them personally. So I might as well go ahead and heal people of sickness the long way. It will help when I have to displace the bacteria and the like, only to have to do it a few at a time, and that will give me more time to figure what else the germs can do now instead of make people sick.

But I think the fact of the matter is that once I had fixed all the tortured people, I would need to go ahead and fix the governments, too, or else they would go back to torturing people while I was healing the sick, and then I would have to start all over.

So I would probably go ahead and perfect all human governments. Then I would have some help, for instance, in rounding up the sick to heal them later, and with abolishing poverty when the time came.

The perfecting of human governments I would definitely accomplish by a visit to each place. There would be a meeting with each government and I would judge and punish the wicked and then the rest of the government would swear to follow your guidance, Sister, or else the guidance of the Alien Being. On occasion I might have to abolish a government rather than perfect it, but that would be all right. A new government would come along to take the place of the old one, and then I could perfect that government instead. I do not believe this whole job should take more than a few weeks since I will be able to take jets and visit more than one country in a day.

After that would come a long time of healing the sick and getting rid of disease. I believe this should be the topic of an entirely different paper. I would leave about two years for this.

You will agree that I have now gone a long way. Under my plan people are now free of disease and torture and bad government. This is ninety percent of the issue.

I would then pause to do something about the name "Peggy." I see no reason it should go on being the nickname for Margaret forever. I would choose a more euphonious name for myself. The name I would choose is a secret, though I did whisper it to the Alien Being the first time you introduced me to it.

A person who is going to carry out all these plans is going to see some pretty horrible things, like open sores and gouged-out eyes and disembowelments and starved-to-death babies. But I know in my heart I can be strong enough for this kind of work. To prepare myself, I have begun to watch the nightly news as well as shows like *Cops*, *Rescue 911*, *Jerry Springer*, *When Animals Attack*, and the surgery channel on cable. It is no coincidence that these are the only shows my dad likes to watch, besides football. He especially likes to watch the rescues on *911*, partly because of the "jaws of life." We watch them together and I no longer make faces even at the bloodiest parts, when they use the jaws of life to rip open an automobile accident and you see the horrible condition of the victims. I think it is good for my dad for me to spend time with him like this. But sometimes I get infected with his strange ideas and that is when I get most discouraged about the subject of fixing the whole world and everything in it.

The poverty will be the hardest part to work on, I think, because even the nicest people are willing to be rich and have more money than others. People just do not see anything wrong with having a lot of money.

For instance, when my dad sees a poor person, he is apt to spit. My grandmother, on the other hand, will spy a woman using food stamps in the grocery, and she will say, in her loud old voice that everybody can hear, "Well, she could at least use her food stamps to buy her some soap and keep herself clean. She could get her a bar of soap sure enough."

Mama says the poor you will have with you always, and I have heard Father Tilman say that too, Sister, so I wonder if it is just something people have accepted. I believe this is a question we should ask the Alien Being the next time we visit. Do they have poor Aliens on Zuta?

These are the kinds of attitudes a policy on poverty would have to deal with. I myself would take a radical approach, such as, I would equalize the money in all the bank accounts and give people extra cash in their pockets and I would erase everybody's memory of who had been rich or poor, so that, for instance, when you met a Rockefeller or a Guggenheim you would no longer secretly expect them to pay for your coffee and Danish. I believe this is the only approach that would work. And even then, watch out. People would almost immediately start getting richer and poorer than each other once again.

Maybe I could also at the same time correct people's attitudes inside their heads on this topic, but I think even a being of godlike power should refrain from altering what people think, however tempting it may be to do a nip and tuck here and there. I do hope you and the Alien Being agree with me on this.

The nice part is, once I got the whole system going, I would have more and more time to perfect things, so that, over time, I could probably make it so the poverty wasn't ever as bad as it used to be. Old folks would hang around the parks telling stories about when people were really really poor back in the old days. Not like today when everybody has it so soft. Shaking their fists at the breezes.

To summarize, the most systematic approach is the one that would work the best in terms of making the world a better place. I would first eliminate torture, then I would perfect all governments and eliminate sickness, disease, and poverty, in that order. It is possible I might have to compromise on the poverty but I would do my best. This is the most practical approach I can think of to fix the world.

I would like you please to tell the Alien Being how much I appreciate him taking an interest in us here at St. Jude's of the Rock Catholic Academy for Girls. I believe it goes without saying that I am honored to be the one who was chosen for this metamorphosis and I promise that when I am nearly all-powerful I will still be the same cheerful person. Suzanne O'Flannagan put in a good plan too and I am sorry she cannot come with me but I think the Alien Being is right, if there were two of us all-powerful ones, we would only fight. I cannot thank you enough for introducing me to the Being, and you know that I will always do my best to serve him, or her, or it, with a good spirit. (Though like I said, I do not intend to be called Peggy by just anyone; however, I will make an exception in the case of you and Father Tilman.) I hope that you will explain all this to my mother and dad. I look forward to seeing you again when we return from the planet Zuta and I begin to exercise my new powers. Best regards, Margaret Ann Hammacker, Ruler of Earth.

UNBENDING EYE

SEEING Roger Dennis at all again was the surprise, much less finding him in a bar on Chartres Street that I visited nearly every evening. I had heard he was dead some time ago. As I remembered the story, he died suddenly in an emergency room in Canada after some kind of accident the details of which I had forgotten, having listened at the time with only a polite modicum of attention, since I had not kept up with Roger after college. Yet here he was in my neighborhood bar where I came most evenings after supper, where the bartender had already seen me enter and poured out my favorite Armagnac.

There was no mistaking Roger for anyone else. When I had known him in college, he possessed a singular, odd beauty that drew others to him, the face of Helen but made masculine, pale blue eyes, dark hair, lips like ripe fruit. We had shared a couple of classes in New Testament Greek. For a while I studied vocabulary with him, and we debated pronunciation and drilled each other in the conjugation of present tense verbs. In appearance he had aged since then, but not in such a way as to change him much. So when I saw him sitting by the window on a stool I thought to myself, well, it must have been somebody else who died, because here he is.

I took my brandy to join him, of course, thinking nothing peculiar, only that I ought to remember who told me he was dead so that I could correct the misinformation. But when I approached, he looked up at me and registered a jolt of shock; then he composed himself and greeted me with a handshake. But I could see that my appearance had frightened him. We greeted each other and the fear passed, but after we had spoken a few moments he began to glance at the window and then suggested we move to the back of the bar, where there were a few stools in a shadowed corner. There he seemed more relaxed and we spoke pleasantly on ordinary topics, what we had done since school, when we had last seen each other, the pains we had shared translating passages from Paul's epistles. I sipped the Armagnac and let my nostrils linger in the rich aroma while he mentioned that he was looking to get out of the country on a ship here in New Orleans but had not yet booked any passage. My family had any number of ships in port at the moment, some cargo vessels with room for a few passengers, and when I mentioned this, his eyes lit and he nearly lunged toward me to take my arm. "I need to leave the country very quietly," he said. "Can you help me do that?"

I assured him that no one was in a better position to offer such help than I, and at his deep relief I was struck by the strangeness of the situation, that here he was alive when I had heard otherwise, yes, very much alive but needing to exit the country in secret. "Of course I'll help you," I said, "but you've made me very curious. Not just this business." I waved my hand a bit, feeling the liquor, but instinctively I kept my voice low. "I heard you were dead years ago."

He stared into his glass and said nothing.

"You must admit that it's very curious. And now here you are, wanting to sail away without a trace. Unless it really wasn't you I heard about. Unless I'm mistaken, unless it was someone else."

Something narrowed in his gaze, as if he were coming suddenly to focus, all of him drawn to a point. When he looked into my eyes I felt the gaze so far inside me that I shivered. "No," he said, "it was me who died," and ordered another drink, and when it arrived he told me this story.

●　　●　　·

I will begin, he said, with the last scene I remember before I died: I was looking up from the emergency room examining table, listening to the doctor order a tomographic scan of my head, and somehow I knew, I must have heard, the fact that I had been injured. I had fallen down steps, crashing headfirst against a wall. I remember the fall only as a flash of something rushing toward me and a force on the top of my head. Nausea rushed through me in the emergency room and I felt my head pounding and my stomach heaved and someone propped me up and helped me to vomit and something split inside my skull and everything after that was hazy.

I woke up in another room, lying with a sheet pulled over my face. The thought occurred to me that I might be dead, in a morgue, maybe, and I lay there for a long time while a square of sunlight moved slowly down my body. I lay still until the room began to get dark. Feeling as if I had been drugged. Near sundown for some reason the thought occurred to me that I should try to move, and I found I could move and sat up and looked out the window. A view of pink light in the sky and the tops of some fir trees, more tops of trees stretching away on all sides. Hill country.

While I was lying under the sheet I had thought vaguely I would find myself in a hospital but now I saw quite clearly I was in some other kind of place. I was sitting on a hospital bed, it was true, and there was some monitoring equipment beside me. On either side of my bed rolling screens blocked my view. I sat up and faced the window with the emptiness of the room behind me, all silence, a stillness that struck me as eerie. My head began to throb.

When I touched my head I remembered that I had fallen and hurt myself but at this point my head had been shaved and there was not a wound to be found on it. But still I had the pounding headache—that was the last thing I remembered—so I lay down again and the throbbing subsided. At the back of my head something plucked at the fabric of the pillow and I touched the skin at the base of my skull, a small round hardness there, not a blood clot but plastic, it felt, like the cap on a catheter. Worrying at it with my finger, I lay quietly till my head stopped hurting and I could breathe calmly again.

Presently I smelled an odor in the room and slowly stood. Pervasive in the air, as if a gas had been discharged. The doors and windows appeared to have been carefully sealed; the room had never been designed as airtight, but someone had attempted to make it so. The throbbing surged in my head but not so fiercely this time, and soon subsided. A long narrow room, many beds, an aisle down the center, walls of a nondescript brown tile. As I have been all my life, I was conscious then of the need to remain calm, but for the first time, I reached a state of quietude without any effort, even as I surveyed the two rows of beds, maybe twenty in all.

The beds were all separated by rolling screens, and each was attended by the same type of monitoring equipment. On each of the beds lay a body, covered by the same sort of white sheet that I held to my waist at the moment. As I walked slowly down the center aisle, I could make out the peak of each nose cutting across each face. Perhaps, gazing at these bodies, I felt a bit colder, though only for a moment.

So I had been correct in my first impression. This was a morgue, since these people were all dead.

The nearest of the bodies was a woman, perhaps in her late twenties, naked as I was, head shaven like mine. Her body had no odor of decay, and she had died in rather good shape with no obvious wounds. She was well preserved. When I lay my fingers between her breasts, the moist cleavage yielded no trace of a heartbeat. The flesh was soft and slightly cool. I leaned close to her, and smelled a sweet aroma rising out of her, the same over her head as over her torso, her feet. As if she had been dipped in a bath.

It occurred to me that she had died a beautiful woman. I say occurred to me because the thought did not enter naturally, as it would have in the past. I gazed down at this woman, took the sheet off her, to see all her nakedness at once. Feeling hardly anything at all.

Without hurry I examined all the bodies, uncovering their faces, their torsos, sometimes letting the sheet drop to the floor beside the bed. Once, when I noted that the sheet covering a particular body was completely white and clean, I exchanged it for my own, which was marred by several dull brown stains, perhaps old blood stains that had been laundered many times but nevertheless remained clearly visible. This left bare the fair-complexioned man whose grave I was robbing, in a sense, his bronze fingers curled gracefully against his thigh, soft, the shadow like a Chinese ideogram. I felt nothing for this man, any more than I had for the lovely dead woman several beds away, and I was certain he no longer minded much of anything, including the fact that I wanted his sheet.

Nineteen bodies I counted, ten female and nine male. All appeared approximately the same age, which was approximately my age; all were in rather good physical condition, as I was; all had the same sweet smell, except me, who smelled his own ordinary body odor. All had shaven heads.

I would not say I was surprised by any of this, but there was one thing more. I chose a young woman. Whatever had been added to these bodies to preserve them in this way, with this light scent of roses, of jasmine, of honeysuckle, had left the flesh soft, if cool, and rendered the joints limber, so that it was easy to raise her head. I had expected some hindrance of rigor mortis and was relieved, though puzzled, for she was clearly dead, but it was as though she he died only a moment ago.

At the back of her head, just at the base of her skull but slightly off center, a neat square in blue had been tattooed onto the skull and at the center of the square nested a small white cap. I could not remove the cap in the one easy tug I gave it, and to do more seemed morbid.

Replacing her head gently on the bed, I covered her with the sheet again, and then, because I hardly knew anything else to do, I replaced the sheets over all the bodies, till everything was just as it had

been before. As I was finishing this task, I heard a door open, followed by the sound of a number of people entering. Overhead, rows
of fluorescent lamps flooded the room with harsh light. Though I
had been able to see perfectly well without it, every detail.

I turned unhurriedly to face the people who were waiting,
drawing the sheet more closely around me, determined to make the
best appearance possible. A group of men and women, dressed in
dark suits or lab coats, approached me. Now one of them stepped
forward, an older woman, a long, crooked nose, bad skin, a smell of
too much powder, and she was raising her hands to greet me, to tell
me what had happened to me, but I was tired already.

●   ●   ·

The doctors were very proud of their project, however, and so, after I had dressed in the awful clothes they offered me, they took me
to a conference room with all the latest electronic equipment, including a projection screen that they could all write on at the same
time, when they could get the electronic pens to work. Videocon-
ferencing cameras in the four corners of the room, in case they
should need to videoconference with somebody, and microphones
at each chair, small and round. So much extremely modern equipment housed in what looked like an old hospital from the forties,
plaster walls and tile wainscoting, crank windows and steam radia-
tor pipes. In the conference room they introduced themselves;
there were, I learned, five doctors and four security people, as they
termed themselves. Their chief, the woman who had spoken to
me, introduced herself as Dr. Carla Lucas, and after we had been
served coffee and sweet doughnuts, nearly inedible, she proceeded

to deliver a brief lecture on the nature and purpose of this apparently dilapidated installation: research into a means of suspending the effects of decay on recently deceased bodies, an attempt to extend the viability of the organs for transplant or other use. The research was based on early success with the use of hyperoxygenated compounds injected into the corpses of laboratory animals just after death. This had led them to an unexpected bit of serendipity: certain laboratory mice when freshly dead and preserved in this way had actually come back to life when stimulated internally with an electrical charge. The viable percentage had increased dramatically when a preparation that included a massive number of fetal neural cells was injected directly into the dead mouse's brain, and when the tissues were kept under one and one-half atmospheres of pressure in a mix of gases more rich in oxygen than the usual.

I endeavored to listen to the details but could not for the life of me take my eyes off the doctors, all of whom were dressed in quite shabby clothes, tattered sleeves and worn elbows, holes in the soles of their shoes. The security people were also wearing really awful outfits, some sort of blend of fabrics that ballooned out stiffly from the thighs, like jodhpurs. The doctors were endeavoring to convince me that this research was being conducted by some branch of our Canadian government and the security people were agreeing with this, but I had great difficulty believing that federal officials could be so badly dressed. They looked as though they had all been hired by the local school board.

I should try to remember all of what they told me in this conference room because I have a feeling it was important, but for the life of me, little of it made any impression on me whatsoever. I understood that they were very excited by the fact that I was walking around, breathing, and that they meant to do a lot of tests on me to make sure my body was functioning as it had before I died.

Dr. Lucas flashed on the screen a diagram of the human skull, and her hand hung slackly at the point at the base of the skull labeled "Point Alpha," with some attempt at grandeur. The researchers had injected their neural stew into this point, and this had apparently jumpstarted the brain—my brain, she meant—while at another insertion at Point Beta, into a vein in the chest near the heart, they injected a small, ingeniously devised matrix of electrically charged proteins, a kind of organic lightning bolt, she said (and had said this phrase many times before, I intuited, from her pleased expression). This biological battery was designed to lodge along the heart wall and send electrical pulses through the muscle, stimulating the heart to beat. As it had done, in my case. There was more, but I was never good with very many polysyllables at once.

At a certain point the lecture stopped and they were waiting for something. I studied Point Alpha carefully, no less expectant than they. After a moment, Dr. Lucas asked, "Do you have any questions, Mr. Dennis?"

They had been waiting for me. To show some interest. Smiling politely, I shook my head. "No."

The doctors all seemed mildly surprised, and the security people appeared particularly put out. Dr. Lucas, however, gave me a patient, motherly look. As a scientist, she could afford to be generous to me, a layman. "You have understood everything, just as I have explained?"

"Yes, you've been very clear."

She adjusted her reading glasses. "I'm glad to hear it. I was afraid my explanation was too technical."

Simply to reassure her, I said, "Oh no, you've been so helpful." I was sitting at the conference table, trying to appear cheerful, but they were all watching me as if I were saying something wrong. "I suppose I do have one question. How long has it been since I died?"

Dr. Lucas consulted with one of her colleagues, a man with a lot of papers and a palm computer, who needed someone to repeat my name to him, and I heard it, my name, with such a curious detachment. "Roger Dennis." After some checking he was able to announce, with complete satisfaction, that I had been dead about two years, preserved by the hyperoxygenated refrigerant and held in a hyperbaric chamber till the recent procedure had been performed, the various injections with the oxygen-rich gas, which had proven so successful.

"We can't preserve a body much longer than two years, even with the gamma serum," Dr. Potter continued, "so it was a good thing for you we were ready."

"I was getting a little ripe, was I?"

He tittered nervously, and they all looked at one another, as if they wanted to laugh but were uncertain.

Dr. Lucas still smiled at me, but I detected a rising level of discomfort in her stiff expression. "I must say, I find your reaction to all this to be very unexpected."

"My reaction?"

"You hardly show any surprise at all. And yet you're alive again, after dying."

"Well, I don't remember much about being dead."

They laughed a bit at that, then the room got silent. Dr. Lucas was still watching me. To console herself, she entered into another long explanation, about the need for further tests, for, as it turned out, they were puzzled by the fact that I was the only one of the twenty dead people to wake up. "Dead subjects," as she termed them. So many more tests would be needed on me, and on the failures as well, and she hoped I would be willing to undergo them. "We have a mission, now that we know our technique can be successful. We need to know why it is that you've come back to life, the only one of twenty."

"But have I come back to that?" I asked.

Poor dears, all puzzled again. I should not have been so smug, I suppose; it would haunt me later.

"Back to what?" Dr. Lucas asked.

"To life. I only mean to ask if you're sure that's what this is."

● ● ·

My question hardly ruffled them, I think, though it would echo for a while. The philosophical underpinnings of our situation never interested them, that I could detect, then or later. We were finished with the briefing, I could go. One of the doctors conducted me to my rooms, which were actually rather pleasant, if nondescript. A small bedroom adjoined a small sitting room, with a bathroom tucked between. Windows with old-fashioned, and rather yellowed, venetian blinds. Clean down to the last corner, a state so conspicuous I wondered if they were worried I might be susceptible to bacteria or contagion, me in my freshly dead state. Or post-dead, rather.

Dr. Potter stopped by to suggest that I rest, as in the morning I would be having several imaging studies, under the supervision of Dr. Lucas herself. He asked me some questions, took my vital signs, noted the strength of my reflexes, all the while making neat notations into his computer. Dr. Potter expressed his hope that I understood the importance of the work in which he and his colleagues were engaged.

"I believe I am engaged in it, too," I said.

"What? You are, of course, you are. And you play the most vital role of all. One might say that, even."

"I believe you could say that."

He lingered another moment and finally came to the point. "Do you remember your past life? Do you know who you were?"

"I was—I suppose I am—Roger Dennis, a systems analyst for a small software company in Montreal. Is that right? I could tell you some of my memories but I doubt you would know whether they're correct or not."

"No, I suppose I wouldn't."

"Then I don't understand your question."

"I was simply curious because you've expressed no interest in any of that. Your life. Your family."

"But I'm dead, as far as they're concerned."

"Yes."

I turned away from him, lay on the bed. "Then I really don't see the point." And I didn't. I felt nothing. Not for my mother, my sisters, the woman I had been dating. It was as if the memories had grayed.

Dr. Potter retired soon after, when the old man Farley came with my dinner. Setting the tray on a table in the living room, nodding to the security guard posted at my door, Farley showed his name badge (for what, I don't know) but refused to look me in the eye. I suppose he knew I had been dead and was uncomfortable about it. Not a scientist, I guessed, but someone rather ordinary, though he had remarkable blue eyes and shaggy, heavy brows hanging over them.

The meal appeared to have been prepared carefully, but I found I had no taste for it at all until the hot foods cooled. Even then I could not stomach the small beef steak. I ate the leafy salad and the over-boiled broccoli. Presently the old man came to take the plate away, still refusing to look at me, snatching the tray and scurrying away, and I wished, vaguely, for a pair of fangs to wear the next time he came in.

Needing no rest, I went for a walk. I wondered if the security person would try to hinder me but she simply fell in beside me. Her presence proved no bother at all, since she said not one word. I was delighted that we might thus avoid all personal tedium and we explored this post of scientific progress as thoroughly as I was allowed, even leaving the building, at one point, to stroll in a courtyard, the moon over the wall, razor wire thrown into silhouette.

The fresh air smelled wonderful and I remarked on it. The security woman said she liked to get out, and I smiled. The stars were fierce. One would have thought that, once outside, my curiosity would have led me to examine this exterior of what had evidently become my prison; but it was only the stars that I cared to watch. Fascinating, thousand upon thousand, teeming, dense, white-hot light drifting from such incomprehensible distances, a particle of light bound all the way from a star into my eye. Pouring untroubled through all that emptiness. I felt something familiar, standing there, gazing upward. Some shiver of feeling passed through me, an echoing loneliness.

I asked the security woman to lead me back to the rooms then, and she did, and I lay in bed all night, staring upward in the dark.

·   •   ●

As it happened, those first examinations stretched into some months. I doubt any human body has ever been better mapped, unless it be one of the virgins of *The 120 Days of Sodom*. The staff of the installation was not large but there must have been forty or fifty people on site. They were all bright, earnest people who dressed very badly, and after a time I came to the conclusion that they were engaged in the search for something almost out of habit, as if this project had been funded once, a long time ago, and continued because nobody had asked about it since. Most of the people here were doctors but I was never sure which of them were medical doctors, though I did soon enough recognize Dr. Stewart as a neurosurgeon by his arrogance and haughty treatment of his peers.

There were certainly enough of them that their complete attention on my limited number of molecules soon proved irksome. I was scanned in a magnet and under radiation, by positron emission, by sound wave; I swallowed radioactive dyes and endured other kinds of contrast imaging studies, the whole panoply available right there in the complex. My image was reconstructed in three dimensions in the various computers in the various rooms and I would lie there, watching the iodine-stained image of my heart beating, the slight ischemic defect in one of the walls, present since I was a child, from a time when I nearly drowned and had to be revived by cardiopulmonary resuscitation. Even granted that some of the equipment appeared outdated, the array of toys these fellows had was impressive. The imaging studies proved only that my body had apparently taken on its normal human functioning once again, in spite of the fact that I had suffered a brain concussion and death and had been preserved by means of something called gamma serum, followed by refrigeration for nearly two years.

When I chafed at all this attention, however, I did note that my fate was superior to that of the nineteen corpses who had failed to resurrect, all of whom were undergoing the most extensive autopsies imaginable, under supervision of a team of pathologists led by Dr. Shiraz.

They were looking in the wrong place, and I already suspected the truth, but I had no reason to say so. I no longer felt present in a living world; I felt I had settled into something else. This proved more than an illusion. Nothing they did hurt me in the least, or caused me the slightest discomfort, not when they sampled liver or lung tissue, not when they cored my bone for marrow. I said nothing. If offered a painkiller I took it, but I felt nothing from it, except a temporary sense of concealment.

At night, in my small suite, I lay on the bed watching the shadowed ceiling. No longer sleeping, though I only revealed this to the doctors when they were performing their sleep studies. Had I always been an insomniac? No, I had never had any trouble of that kind. But my medical records, which they had apparently obtained, indicated that I had asked for sleeping pills on several occasions from my primary care doctor. Because I liked to take sleeping pills, I said. Very pleasant.

They gave me more sleeping pills. They gave me injections. They could knock me unconscious, they learned. But they could not put me to sleep.

This caused some consternation, particularly for the neurologist Dr. Shabahrahmi, who performed various scans of my brains, some lasting for hours, to determine exactly what type of brainwave activity I had when unconscious. He found nothing determinate, except that I never slept.

I often rested, however, lying in the bed dressed as if I were sleeping, staring up at the darkness, at the ceiling, at whatever was there.

At the end of these first examinations, nothing had been determined that could differentiate me from my dissected fellow specimens, except that I had, for some reason, gotten up from bed when I was supposed to, and the others had not. The mystery had, in fact, deepened, since it was clear that, along with rising from the dead, I had undergone some kind of change. I had lost the need for sleep. But these learned people could not determine why.

I had lost other appetites, and these were duly noted and, in the secondary phase of their study of me, tests were performed on these missing appetites as well. I had asked that the dietitian no longer allow the old man to serve me any meat, and, after a while, I lost all appetite for cooked food. I ate fresh fruits and vegetables. The doctors tested me by feeding me meat, which I would promptly vomit up, and they would scurry to do tests on the vomit, to determine what type of stomach acid was present in it, and to look at my stomach, to see if they could learn why my stomach was suddenly rejecting this food. But again, the tests showed no conclusive results, vomit that was like anyone else's vomit, feces that was like anyone else's feces, nothing to lead them anywhere, only the fact that I had changed in some way, for some reason that eluded them.

It was suggested that my change in eating habits might be the result of some psychological changes, and that these might require study, but there were no psychiatrists or psychologists on the staff of the project, and these branches of science were not held in high regard. Those ideas were never pursued.

●   ●   ·

A week or so passed during which no tests were conducted and nearly all my time was my own. I remember speculating that perhaps they were abandoning this line of research and would set me free. Looking back on that now, it seems such an innocent thought, particularly for a man who had already died once and ought to know better. But a certain innocence still remained to me. I was aware that many discussions were going on around me during this quiet interlude, but I ignored them. With hours to myself, I sat for long intervals in the courtyard at night, staring up at the stars, watching them wheel slowly overhead. Gazing upward into the face of something cold and unknowable.

Dr. Lucas called me to her office at the end of the week, and the security guard, Taquanda, the same woman as on my first day, escorted me to her. They had kept up the practice of the continuous security escort and guard for my quarters though I had never shown the least inclination to escape, so I had gotten to know some of my guardians by name. Dr. Lucas beckoned me inside and closed the door. She always did her makeup very badly, sloppy lipstick and crooked mascara, and today was wearing something awful, a knit dress that clung to her lumpish body in all the wrong places; she seemed even more hideous than if she had been naked, so that the interview was conducted, on my part, in a state of horror, as though I were conversing with Grendel's mother. "Can you guess why I've called you tonight?"

"I suppose I could try. You've been reassessing your results this past week and there's been a lot of disagreement as to what you ought to do next. But now you've come to some decision."

"Yes, we have." She patted her hair, drab, thin stuff, no shape. At that moment, I understood I would never be going home. Something about the indifference of her ugliness, none of the gentle peace of homeliness. "We'll be taking another line of research starting tomorrow."

I accepted the information without any show of interest, and she waited, and finally said, "You really aren't at all curious about what we're going to do, are you?"

"You're not going to let me go?"

"No, of course not."

I shrugged. "Then the answer is, no, I'm not curious as to what you're going to do."

She appeared startled by my statements and leaned back in her chair. Tapping that crooked nose with a sharp fingertip. "We can't let you go, unfortunately; you're our only hope."

"To bring back more people like me. From the dead."

"Surely you understand the value of what we're doing."

I gave no sign that I understood anything at all, and finally, exasperated, she began to clean her eyeglasses with fierce little motions of her hands. "Well, I don't have anything more to say than that. We'll be trying another line of research starting tomorrow. I wish you the best of luck."

"You do?"

"Yes, of course I do." She spoke vehemently, as though I had challenged her humanity on some consequential ground.

"Well, then, I assume I'll need it," I said, and left her office and went back to my rooms.

I ate my dinner, an apple and two bananas, some orange slices, raw carrots, even a raw potato, which was good to keep and nibble. I have no idea which of the fruits or vegetables contained the preparation called Serum Omega, the composition of which no one ever discussed with me, since they were ashamed of its existence. I understood from the strange sensation, the tingling, in all my limbs, that perhaps the doctors were beginning their work earlier than announced. I who had not needed sleep in all these months felt a slow lethargy seep through me, my limbs heavy. What kind of poison kills the body but does not damage it? They came for me before I had completely lost consciousness, lost life, but by then I was paralyzed, and simply felt them stirring around me, dragging me onto a stretcher, wheeling me down the dull tiled corridor. The last thing I remember, in a room that seemed suddenly familiar, was a tingling at the base of my skull, where the little cap had waited, all this time, in case it should be needed again.

●   ●   ·

This time I surfaced in a glare. A light hung just above me, a fierce, round light, and I could not see so much as feel, and the light was not so much a brightness as an insistent gaze transfixing me from a distance infinitely remote from me, out where existence is the only thing there is, out there so far away . . .

A dream? I never woke from it, I surfaced inside it, not as if I were waking but rather descending from a height. I became aware of where my body was and then I was inside it, but the distance seemed greater than before. I was aware of the room, the same clerestory windows, the square of sunlight traveling along the sheet that covered me. Not the same sheet, this one snow white. As before, still bodies lay in the beds on either side of me and along the opposite wall. The motionless sheets shone faintly white, and the sweet smell was almost more than I could bear. I quickly checked the bodies as before, and this time I found one of them breathing, not strong enough to pull the sheet down from her face, but breathing nevertheless, so I pulled it down, and, as I bent over, she looked at me with a complete coldness, utter contempt. She closed her eyes and turned her head away.

She continued to breathe for a while, long enough for the doctors to arrive. They were excited, of course, and rushed her off to revive her further, if they could, though by the time they wrestled her onto a stretcher her breathing was already slowing. She died, or faded, a few minutes later, just down the hall.

While they were studying her they left me alone, except to draw blood and samples of other tissue; her they dissected, sampling her in every way possible, with every type of biopsy pincer and core needle, till at the end of their studies her body was completely exploded into ten thousand pieces, all preserved in formaldehyde in offices up and down the corridors. I used to wonder which pieces of tissue floating in cloudy jars were her, in the later weeks, after they could derive no more pleasure from carving her up into even smaller slices, or mounting slices of her onto slides. Within weeks they returned their attention to me.

They studied me again, all the same tests, some even more invasive and uncomfortable than the first battery. At times they looked at me as if they wanted to cut me apart, too, but they were afraid to do it. The cycle of tests went on and on, till again it stopped for a few days, and I waited.

One night in my room I felt the drowsiness run through all my limbs, unnatural to me by that point, since I had not slept in many months; so I knew I was to die again.

Same as before, a burning gaze above me, all I can remember of that time, or place, or whatever it might be called, between my death and wakening again. I lay beneath a fierce eye examining me every moment, and I longed to be removed from its gaze, but I could only lie there while it watched me, ceaselessly . . .

I woke in the same room as before. For the third time I examined rows of bodies. This time no one had responded to any of the serums or gases, only me. The arrival of the doctors was delayed, as it had been each time, and only now did I become in the least curious that they should leave me alone for so long with these dead ones, this sweet smell in the air. From the expressions of Dr. Lucas and Dr. Potter it was clear they understood they had failed again, and now when they looked at me I could only wonder what lay in store.

For a few days I was left in peace. Then Dr. Lucas called me to her office, and I followed with the escort she had sent, into her sitting room with the old-fashioned crank windows, partly rusted near the

top. Like the office of some elementary school principal, the room
was decorated with darkly stained wooden furniture, slatted blinds
with frayed cords, pipes running ceiling to floor, a steam convector
under the window. She was sitting in this office, dressed more taste-
fully this time, a dark, high-waisted dress that helped mask her lack
of discernible shape, even a pair of what were called ear-bobs in my
mother's day, white and round and big. A touch of lipstick. Feeling
quite honored by the care with which she had done her toilet, I took
my seat on the long, wide sofa, straightening a place for myself in the
twists of the chenille throw. I wondered in an offhand way whether
I should be prepared to die tonight, and after a moment while she
finished some notation or other in some computer file or other, I
stated, "So I expect you are preparing another phase of tests."

She lifted a finger to signal that I should wait, tapped the key-
board intently for another few moments, and closed the lid of the
notebook, the whine of the drive dying away. "Please excuse me.
Yes, we have been discussing our next phases." She sagged in the
chair, clearly exhausted. "We're puzzled more and more by our repeated failures in the aftermath of our one complete success. You,
I mean."

"How many more times do you think you can bring me
back?"

She looked at me quite oddly, quite fixedly. "I really don't
know."

"But you'll keep on till I fail, too."

Her jaw set itself into a strong line. "We'll keep on until we
can understand what is happening in your body that isn't happening with the others. We'll keep on until we succeed."

I must have looked skeptical, for she continued. "We're close, and we know it. The discoveries we've already made are remarkable, really. Tricks even the Egyptians never learned about the preservation of tissue, even its healing after death, as in the case of your brain injury."

"The first time I died, you mean."

"Yes." She waited for a while, then asked, "You don't have anything to say?"

"A question, perhaps."

She leaned forward, as if this were some turning point in our relations. "Go ahead."

"How long was I dead? The first time, I mean. Before your treatment to preserve me."

"We had to give you the first infusion of hyperox before you were taken off life support."

"Before."

"Yes."

I smiled. "You must have a very efficient system for collecting subjects. To find the right kind of dead people, so quickly."

"We had a number of hospitals helping us with the initial part of the study, the part that related to the preservation of organs for reuse. The other portion of our research is confidential. For obvious reasons."

"So when I fell and hit my head, someone called your people as soon as I died. Or just before I died."

"Something like that." She seemed perplexed, then irritated. "Are you implying some sort of impropriety? We aren't killing anyone. We didn't steal your body out of a morgue. Your own next of kin gave us permission to use you in the research. I can show you all the paperwork if you like."

"That won't be necessary," I said. "How many more of me do you have? In the refrigerator, I mean. How long can you go on?"

She set her mouth in a line. "What we're doing here could be of benefit to billions of people."

"Of course it could." I sighed. "That's all. I only had those questions."

She thought about that for a moment. Relaxed, when my tone changed. "I suppose I had expected you to ask about your freedom."

I laughed, and turned away from her, and laughed again.

She gave me the most chilling look, and I wondered if they had already administered the killing specific, if she had brought me to the office to watch me die this time, to witness the exact moment of my passing.

"When I'm dead," I told her, "before you bring me out of it. There's someone watching me."

She moved her head just slightly. I believe she considered that I might have become unstable in some way, and so I stood and waited in the doorway for a moment.

"Who do you think it is?" she asked.

"I don't know. But it strikes me that maybe someone is there, sending me back to you, over and over again. Keeping me there for a while and then sending me back. Only me."

"Why?"

I shrugged.

But she had heard what I said, and judging by her expression, a vision of the place I was describing arose in her head at that moment, a place in which she was lying suspended in darkness from all sides, darkness and cool air, and above a light, a piercing eye gazing into the center of her. I believe she saw this as I had, hanging in that endless expanse, the feeling of a presence, the unbelievably fierce awareness. She had a look of awe, a whiteness to the eyes, a face of glass, and I said good night to her and she whispered good night to me as Taquanda took me back to my room.

One more time they killed me and I woke under the eye, with the wind of that place scouring through me and the searching of that eye above me, never blinking or moving. A voice in my head, not words, only the voice, notes like music, and then my body closed around me like wet clay and I was lying in the room, alone this time, no other corpses to keep me company. Though perhaps somewhere else, in some other room, two rows of beds, faces under white sheets, a sweet smell in the air. Perhaps the doctors had decided to spare me their failures, at least.

The routine had become settled by now, and that first night when I was alive again, or what they called alive, I was allowed to be on my own while the doctors assessed whatever data they had collected during the resurrection. Since I had always been docile, even inert, the security people had become a bit lax, and the security person with me that night was one of those who had fallen under the influence of Farley the cook, who thought me some sort of monster. She hung back from me when I went for a walk and that provided the avenue of escape I needed. By then I knew the layout of the installation fully, and so I lured her into a part of the building that was sparsely inhabited and I strangled her there.

Curious, that I killed her. I had no plan to do anything of the kind, I meant only to immobilize her in some way, maybe knock her out, but instead I put my bare hands around her neck and squeezed with such force that she was quickly gone, despite some struggles to free herself. I let her drop to the floor and turned away. Let them revive her, I thought.

I escaped the place through the kitchen, where Farley was puttering, whistling something rather tuneless, "Waltzing Matilda," I think; and for a moment I wanted to kill him, too, but I decided it was better to let him go on humming, so that when the doctors learned of my escape he could swear that he had been in the kitchen the whole time, getting their dinner ready, and he hadn't seen me. I slid through the pantry, out the delivery door, and headed into the woods at the edge of the parking lot.

The rest is tedious. I stole a car, I stole some money. I crossed the border into the United States on foot and stole another car and more money. I avoided any more killing, though the thought often occurred to me on my journey. I have driven the long way here. Though I am certain there are people trying to find me, people who already know where I've come. So I need to get on a ship going south, to where the sun beats down more strongly from the center of the sky.

·   ·   ●

When his story began I found it fantastic, but troublesome, and as he continued with it, I myself became quite uncomfortable in the noisy bar. So we interrupted the story to walk to my apartment in the Pontalba building, and he finished the telling of it in my parlor, with the casement windows open and the breezes stirring from the front gallery. He sat there with his white hands in his lap. I knew he expected some response, but I had nothing to offer, the story it-self was so astounding.

"You can't really believe me, of course," he said, after a mo-ment, "but that doesn't matter, as long as you help me."

"Of course I'll help you," I said, "first thing in the morning. We have a ship leaving for Caracas, and I'll get you on that."

He seemed very moved by this, settled back into his comfort-able chair. I thought he might fall asleep but remembered his story and watched, and he never more than blinked his eyes.

I led him back to my room, helped him to undress, lay him on the bed, undressed myself and lay down beside him. I watched him all night, his good body, his firm jaw, his face that I had remem-bered from so long ago. We simply lay there, side by side, and I knew I would remember that night, maybe wish we had made love to one another, wish I had tested whether there was any warmth in him at all. To be able to say later that I had made love to a dead man, or a ghost. He never closed his eyes that I saw, though I drifted off myself, in the wee hours. When I woke the next morn-ing he was lying exactly in the same position, gazing upward at the ceiling, high and shadowed, a place into which only he could see.

The captain of the *Sylvia Moon* did not much like my insis-tence in the morning when I called him, but he finally saw the wisdom of acceding to my wishes when he remembered who I was, or rather, who my family was. My friend Roger Dennis set sail immediately for the northern coast of South America.

I had no more idea then than I do now of what to make of his

story. Some people did come looking for him and landed eventually at the office of my family's shipping concern; they were persis-
tent and remained in New Orleans for some days, but they were
not able to penetrate through all the veils of the company to me,
and therefore I can only speculate as to who they were. But I made
certain they learned nothing of the *Sylvia Moon* or its passenger.

My caution was unnecessary, however. Roger Dennis never
landed at any port. The ship's captain later told me, with some fear
for his future, I expect, that as the ship was crossing the Caribbean,
Roger leapt overboard one noon and drowned. His body was not
recovered. The crew gave him a burial service at sea, my captain
said, and since I alone knew who he was, could I please notify his
family? I promised I would take whatever steps were necessary, and
I did make a trip to Ontario, though naturally I saw nothing at all
of his family. I checked the records of the hospital at which Roger
told me he had died, and after various referrals was able to confirm
his original death. Roger Dennis had perished of head trauma after a fall nearly five years before. As if the paper assurance were not
enough, I made a trip to a cemetery near Montreal, where my uncertainty finally increased to the point that I could credit him what
he had claimed. I can believe his story was true, so far as he himself
knew the truth, now that I have seen his grave.

WENDY

KEEP in mind that I made her, I designed her, from component parts purchased legally and fairly on the open market. She is my creation, body and soul; or, rather, body and manufactured self. We're still litigating the matter of her soul. About eight years old in physiognomy, she is possessed of perfect peach-colored skin and a voluptuous form, the curve of her buttocks and thighs heavy, a light fuzz on the skin of her calves, her lips unnaturally full, pouty. She has eyes the color of gulf waters, a startling blue tinged with violet, her dark curls gathered in a clip behind her head. I designed this flower-tender face, this perfect shape of arms, a touch of dimpled flesh at the elbow, fingers slender and tapered. Wendy is my child, my eight-year-old, and I have strapped her to a table, wide-eyed with fright, tender arms and legs completely still, bound by straps of leather and duct tape to the old hospital stretcher in my session rooms. She is staring at the ceiling, at a particular spot in the ceiling, exactly as I have instructed her to do. Fine golden wires run in and out of her, piercing the silky skin to entwine with her tender nerves, her delicate processes of feeling and sensation. Her entire body is throbbing in anticipation of the pain she is about to undergo. She is Wendy, organic construct, inhabited by the most advanced of artificial intelligences, alive in every sense of the word except for the actuality that she is an artifact, something I have fashioned, a doll of living tissue and artificial sensibility, an object, and I keep her in a complex of rooms in the basement of my large, comfortable house in Sheffield Falls, a suburb of Atlanta.

Wendy's body comes from Gentech Valley Constructs, a corporation in which I own a great number of shares. She was seven years in the making, cloned from commercially available, publicly licensed DNA, her body brainless, like most bodies grown for organ harvest. I purchased a commercially grown child's brain to install in her cranium, added a coil processor at the base of the skull, loaded the requisite programs and added some other hardware attachments, at the same time wiping out certain centers of the prefrontal cortex which would tend to cause the development of an organic personality. Wendy's personality is my own creation, or, to be more precise, the creation of Selfware Institute, another company in which I am involved financially; the custom-made personality is installed into her mechanical and organic hardware, overriding any tendency of the living parts of her to develop independently into some sort of "person." Wendy, my daughter, is a body grown in a tank, a brain bought on the open market, and the best software money can buy.

"Do you feel anything, Wendy?' I ask, leaning over the table, looking into her eyes, which are swimming with tears, her lips trembling.

She knows better than to answer.

I use the pronoun "she" although my attorney, Rhoda Maximeter, advises against it. Rhoda advises that using this pronoun tends to assign a certain level of humanity to the entity known as Wendy. I counter that people call their dogs "he" and "she" without incurring any legal obligation to recognize a cocker spaniel, for instance, as a person. Dogs do have rights, of course, whereas Wendy, being an object, has none; we settled the issue of her animal status during the life of one of her predecessors. I insist that it is appropriate to call Wendy "she" and to treat her in every respect as a little girl, a child of seven or eight, not because of any right she has to be treated in this way but because her therapeutic value to me is increased by the pretense.

For several years I have been involved in lawsuits to establish my right to construct organic dolls like Wendy and to abuse them as I please. Lately, while my lawsuit is going quite well, my sessions with Wendy have become less satisfying.

Tonight is no different. When I am finished with Wendy, my body trembling, I give her the command to deactivate, a few words that send her into sleep. In this mode, her hardware will perform a complete reset of all systems, flushing any residual memory out of her operating system, so that when we begin our next session, I can be certain that I am abusing a completely rebooted copy of Wendy's factory-installed behavior protocols. My attorneys insist on this step as necessary to prove Wendy is the doll I claim her to be; they, like nearly everyone else—like me, sometimes—are under compulsion to believe that she is secretly trying to become human.

Tonight the fact that she will remember nothing that has happened between us, nothing that I have done to her, troubles me.

·   •   ●

The rooms in which Wendy is maintained and serviced lie in a windowless underground facility constructed adjacent to my home; I call these rooms the Nursery. My activities with Wendy are conducted under the supervision of a team of physicians, including my psychiatrist, my primary care physician, my neurologist, and several therapists who are attempting to help me control my tendencies toward sexual pathology through use of Wendy as a surrogate for a real child. Full-time nurses watch Wendy around the clock and monitor the status of her organic parts, particularly in the aftermath of my sessions with her, when she may need treatment for injury.

Bridget is the nurse on duty tonight. She's typical of my staff, never certain whether to look me in the eye or not, vaguely ashamed to be in my employ; but, like the others, she has something in her past that prevents her finding a more acceptable job. Bridget killed her own daughter in a drunk-driving accident several years ago, and is lucky to have found any kind of work at all following her prison sentence for manslaughter. Fleshy, thick-waisted, hair faded from red to dun, she shifts nervously in her duty seat, eyeing the monitors that register Wendy's blood pressure, her respiratory rate, her pulse. I have left the curtains closed inside the session room. Bridget glares at me and looks at the monitor. She has been with me through the lives of Wendy's two predecessors, an old friend. Her hostility toward me is palpable.

"Wendy needs you," I say.

She gives a little nod, eyes fiercely fixed on the desktop. There in a gold frame sits a picture of a little girl, dark curls, big eyes, nuzzling a red plastic dinosaur in a pink mouth, the toy clutched in a pink hand, Bridget's dead daughter, last seen with her skull smashed in the passenger seat of Bridget's Toyota Camry. At moments like this present one, when I have finished a session with Wendy and must face Bridget, I focus on this image, Bridget reeling drunk next to her daughter's broken body. It helps me not to make too much of my own shame.

"Is she hurt?" Bridget asks, flushed, lips pursed together.

"Not badly."

"Did you turn off the pain protocol?"

"Yes."

She takes a quick, harsh breath. I can read all that she would like to say to me in the set of her shoulders, the tension of her neck. The moment when she remembers how badly she needs this job is the clearest of all; her shoulders sag and she bows her head, no longer able to look at the picture of her little girl. She asks, "Do you need me to call one of the doctors? For you, I mean?"

Her tone is far gentler than I deserve. "No," I say. "I'm sure Dr. Warner is outside. I'll find him."

At the door, even though I am no longer watching her, I can picture her angry posture, thick body rising from the chair, stepping

into Wendy's room, certain to be wondering what she'll find there
this time.

· • ●

Were it not for the Wendy doll and her predecessors, I might have
begun to abuse real children by now. My personality is publicly
listed as one of the dozen or so types that incline to this kind of
practice. My DNA contains several of the genes that have been
linked to serial killers and other violent offenders, and my psychi-
atric profile confirms abusive interest in young girls. In order to
enjoy this illicit pleasure legally, I must make certain that my Wendy
dolls and their increasingly lifelike successors are never allowed to
enjoy legal status as human beings. I am currently in court to prove
that Wendy is a machine.

Because I manufactured Wendy without making any attempt
to hide what I was doing, freely using my rather vast family for-
tune, I have become a target of advocates demanding human rights
for organic constructs and other entities with artificial intelligence.
I have been sued by liberal and conservative alike, countless times,
each legal decision defining a new region of this murky area of the
law, beginning with a lawsuit that proved conclusively that Wendy's
predecessor Emily could not be considered an animal and therefore
enjoyed no animal rights. This precedent was important in reaf-
firming the principle that bodies grown for organ harvest were not
protected under animal cruelty laws.

The current lawsuits are aimed at establishing legal rights for
Wendy on the basis of her artificial sentience. We are litigating toward a legal definition of a human being and whether or not any

kind of created sentience should enjoy the same status. In this fight
I have many allies, and many opponents.

My most effective legal opponent, Lisa Santa Maria St. James-
Aislund of the Third Millennium Foundation for Human Rights
and Beyond, has hired a fleet of assistant attorneys in elegant dark
suits to help force me to give Wendy up for adoption by loving,
caring parents. Lisa Santa Maria wears couture suits in the most elegant shades of beige, mauve, lavender, teal, gray, pearl, oyster, and
ecru, her hair pulled tightly into a bun, her genetically perfect body
tucked precisely into the clothing to generate maximum advantage
from her packaging. Frighteningly beautiful, she has only to lift her
chin slightly to engender a chorus of photographer's clicks. For
years, when I had my daughter Olive, Santa Maria tried to convince the district attorney to pursue felony charges of child mo-
lestation against me, but my own battalion of barristers, headed by
the busty Rhoda Maximeter with her generously round propor-
tions, always managed to frighten the state away from pursuit of
action.

Arguing as friends to my defense are those entities one might
expect: creators of artificial intelligences and smart machines, their
corporate owners having no desire to see their products granted legal status as people. But my list of allies also includes, against all in-
stinctive reason, a legion of churches and conservative groups
determined to help me prove that nothing manufactured by hu-
mans should be called human. Only God can make a soul. These
co-litigants include the Conservative Christian Coalition, the Sally
Randall Foundation, the Muslim Liberty Council, the Jewish Anti-
Cloning League, the Anti-Homosexual Ecumenical Opposition,

and a host of others. In their view, there can be only one acceptable
outcome to this trial. Wendy must be declared a machine. As for
me, in time I will be gathered to God's punishment one way or the
other; one more lost sinner, in the end, makes hardly any difference.
I am not religious, but I am glad for the backing. My defense team
and I ignore the fact that many of these groups, including the Sally
Randall Foundation, have often sued Gentech Valley and my family's other holdings, attempting to stop our organ farming as an
abomination in the sight of God.

The trial is coming to a close; reporters and members of the
media are swarming; the eyes of the world are on our little
Sheffield Falls courthouse. This decision, it appears, will be defini-
tive, provided that it survives all the appeals that are likely to be
filed after it is rendered. After this, the courts will have spoken, and
the only further remedy would be a change in the law.

Today is pleasant, a spring day, the scent of jasmine and honeysuckle drifting from the open windows of the courthouse. On the
witness stand, under questioning by the right honorable Lisa Santa
Maria, I am cool and unruffled in my Delorean suit.

"When did you first begin to abuse your daughter?" asks Santa
Maria.

Rhoda heaves her large bulk to her feet, bolstered by a good
push from one her associates. "Your Honor, how many times must
I tender the same objection to the court? My client has no natural
daughter."

"But he himself refers to Wendy as—"

"Objection sustained, Miss Santa Maria. You will refer to
Wendy as 'the object Wendy' or simply by its designation."

For the benefit of the judge, she makes a cynical face in my direction and repeats her question in corrected form. When did I begin to abuse the object Wendy?

"I do not abuse the object. It is maintained properly in every way. It's well fed and housed and given good physical care."

"It is true that you torture Wendy, is it not?"

"The object Wendy was designed to be used in simulations of torture, yes."

"Simulations?"

"You can't torture a machine."

"Wendy has an organic body, correct?"

"Yes, she does. I purchased it—"

"Thank you. She has a human body. This body feels pain."

"No. This body undergoes biochemical changes in response to stimuli. It takes a person to feel pain."

"Or an animal."

"Yes, an animal."

"Wendy does have an animal body."

"One of the components of the machine is an organic body, yes."

"This animal body is capable of providing a stimulus to the brain that a person would feel as pain, is that not correct?"

I have rehearsed these arguments many times in many courtrooms. "Yes. But in Wendy's case, her brain is nonfunctional in the personality centers, where a person would feel stimuli. These areas of the brain have been atrophied and their function rerouted to a Steinberg coil installed in the rear of her skull near the spinal juncture. The feeling function is handled by mechanical processors.

The system is periodically rebooted so that no continuously functioning self can evolve even in the mechanical layers of the toy."

"Toy?"

I am not supposed to use that word, but I have let it slip, perhaps deliberately. I am calm, in spite of the lapse, and look Santa
Maria in the eye. Her stunning facial symmetry is pointless; she's
far too old for a pervert like me. I say, "Wendy is, essentially, an
elaborate toy."

This case is being tried before the judge; there is no jury. The
judge is Adwhiri Faheed Jarman of the Seventeenth Circuit Federal Court in Atlanta; she stirs when she hears this word, "toy." She
is a mother herself, with the requisite two children, both daughters.
Perhaps she is picturing her own child in my hands.

Red-faced, righteous, ineffably gorgeous, Santa Maria purrs in
her most mellifluous voice. "So when you think of this child as a
toy, you don't have to worry about whether she feels pain or not?"

Objections, arguments, a sea of words. The judge keeps her
cool, issues her statements in the clearest tone. Into this noise I
wade, eyeing Rhoda calmly, then turning to the judge. Wearing my
mildest expression, I mean to remind her of her most harmless old
uncle. "I'd like to answer the question, your honor, if I may."

Rhoda is stunned and Santa Maria is smiling.

Judge Jarman, solemn, nods that I may do so.

I speak cautiously, looking into the courtroom but aware that
the judge is my audience. My eyes are large with feeling and I speak
in an earnest voice. "I'm a state-registered personality type known
to be prone to violence against real children, though I have never
acted on these tendencies toward any child. In my case no kind of

therapy can arrest the progression of my illness. Because of my inherited wealth, I have the means to build myself an object that acts as a surrogate and meets my needs. I am under the supervision of doctors and so is the object. Calling Wendy a toy is a further effort to reinforce this process. Using Wendy, I have isolated myself from contact with real human children and have enabled myself to live a normal life without doing anyone harm. In taking all these steps, some of which were enormously time-consuming and expensive, I have acted for the protection of real children in real families."

At the end of my speech, Santa Maria is stunned and Rhoda is smiling. The judge has relaxed a bit, and I would guess that in her mind's eye she is no longer seeing the face of her youngest daughter as I lean over her bed to wrap my hands around her throat. The judge sees, instead, my struggle to maintain some kind of equilibrium, to live some kind of decent life. She sees my search for the good and the beautiful. She has a look of calm concentration that I admire as she listens to Santa Maria's next question. The judge's cheekbones shine.

●　　●　　·

In the Nursery, Bridget is on duty at the desk again, dark circles under her eyes, reading from a supermarket tabloid with a huge blowup of Wendy's face, a picture smuggled out of the Nursery by one of the day nurses, currently unemployed. In the picture Wendy is posing for a portrait of herself, dressed in ruffles and bows like anybody's little girl, her features tender and innocent, something forlorn in her eyes. Bridget scowls at me, jaw set, as I linger at the one-way glass, looking into Wendy's room.

"I won't be closing the curtains tonight," I say.

This is code which means, I won't be having a session with Wendy tonight. Wendy's rooms are soundproofed; I have only to lock the door and close the curtains inside for all the privacy I want.

When I watch Bridget again, I want to note some relaxation, some softening toward me. Tonight I won't be hurting Wendy; doesn't that mean I'm a better person, at least for the moment? But Bridget simply gives a nod, tucks her chin down, fastens her eyes on the tabloid photograph. The soft fuzz of a menopausal beard has begun to cover her chin. She looks as tired as can be.

When I go into the room, Wendy watches me with that look of careful consideration that is her least childish affect. She must sense that tonight is different, that I am edgy, though she can hardly know the reason. While her software is constantly rebooted, her awareness and sensory capacity is much greater than that of a human child, and her computing ability is extraordinary. Her behavior is governed by algorithms purchased from the best experts in artificial behavior. She has a basic program, a life story, built into her hardware; she has several, in fact, in case I should tire of one or another of our scenarios. Her behavior between reboots is so consistent that the effect is that of a personality. I have been able to ride the line between believing her a real child and knowing her to be an object, but after tonight, the law will be interpreted and a judicial opinion will be on the books. Her status will be fixed.

Wendy as a thinking object commands a good deal of data

concerning herself and her plight; a careless person might consider this to be understanding.

"Reboot," I say, and watch as her eyes glaze, her lower lip trembling. She closes her eyes and the orbs move under the lids, not randomly but in even sweeps back and forth, up and down. She sticks out her pink tongue and retracts it. She flexes her fingers.

She has been reborn again. A calm settles over her features. "Hello, Mr. Desai," she says. This is the default greeting from reboot, designed for public showcases. Wendy in this state is devoid of sensation or fear. She smiles at me in perfect innocence. "Do you want to select from the program?"

"No, Wendy. I just want to talk for a minute."

She is bemused, an expression beyond her years. "To me?"

"Yes, Wendy."

"Is there someone here? Are we doing a demonstration that's not on my schedule?"

"No. We're just talking."

She blinks at me. This version of Wendy has only a basic layer of functionality. Why, then, does she seem apprehensive? "Talking."

"Yes. I thought I might say a few things to you."

Something delicious, something like fear, is evident on her features. Or maybe this is what I am looking for, knowing what I am about to tell her. "Do you want me to store this conversation in hardware?"

"Yes, you may as well."

"Very well, Mr. Desai. Storage protocols are functioning." She looks at me, smile tenuous, lips beaded with sweat.

"I'm very troubled about our future," I say quietly. "I'm very disturbed."

"Disturbed?" Her conversational choices are limited; she defaults to repeating a key word when she fails to understand how to move a conversation forward. But the effect is different, as if tension is building between us, as if she is understanding the thing that is about to happen.

"The judge hands down her ruling tomorrow," I say.

"Judge Adwhiri Faheed Jarman."

"Yes. She decides whether you're legally human."

A flush rises through her skin, and she frowns. "Human."

"Yes." I stroke her soft, damp hair. "Are you in pain?"

This question she understands. "No, Mr. Desai. As you know, in this mode of my function, I do not feel pain."

"Would you like to?"

She shudders, and meets my eye, and looks away.

Is this her protocol, or is this real fear?

I have only to say two words, I have only to say, "Access pain," and her software will open the gates of sensation in her artificial cortical centers. After that, I might do anything. I might put an end to her altogether.

But I stop short. I have already told Bridget I will not close the curtains tonight. Watching Wendy, I can no longer decide whether she is here or not. Surely it is the idea that she is real that drives me to torture her and to abuse her as I do. Isn't it clear that I want to believe she is a person, a real child? Isn't it clear that my life depends on that?

"Deactivate," I say, and she closes her eyes immediately, not a millisecond of hesitation, comfortably machinelike, instantly responsive.

●　　●　　·

I win the judge's ruling on the grounds that I have proven Wendy was assembled from purchased components and that I have taken sufficient safeguards to prevent the development of a human personality in her hardware. This is close to the last gasp of a whole movement, and a ripple of response runs through the polite people in the gallery. Santa Maria looks like something fell on her out of the sky, as if she never considered she might lose, but that has to be performance. The outcome has never really been in doubt.

When I hear the ruling and feel Rhoda's relief, I want to tell her that I almost killed Wendy last night, that I almost sliced her throat after I almost carved my name on her belly, after I almost raped her, after I almost sent volts of pain ripping through her, after I almost filled her with misery. But something changed my mind.

Judge Jarman is watching me but pretending to arrange panes on her flat screen; she is wary again, wondering again. Now that she has made her pronouncement she has her doubts. She suspects I may transform into a monster after all.

I already know Wendy is finished, as far as I'm concerned. She's no good to me any more.

The judge adjusts her robes, making eye contact with no one except her bodyguard as she steps away from her bench through the doorway that springs open at her back. I wonder what her daughter is like; from news reports I already know her younger child is of an age that should appeal to me. I wonder whether I can find a picture of her on the Internet, learn her name, maybe find a way to see her. Waves, first of terror, then of longing, pass through me at the thought. I gather myself together, shake Rhoda's hand, smile for the cameras, and leave the courtroom.

·   •   ●

One last time I visit the Nursery, where Wendy is in her day room running the protocol called "Amuse yourself." This is her most open-ended protocol in which she explores her surroundings, playing with her toys, examining books and pictures. In this mode she is theoretically capable of learning. She looks like any eight-year-old playing in her room, trying to figure out her immediate world. On duty at the nurse desk is one of the day shift staff, indifferent to me and to Wendy. I find myself wishing Bridget were here to glower.

Upstairs, I leave a note behind explaining my decision. There are no choices left. I've already found out where Judge Jarman lives, what school her daughter attends, what she looks like; I've already followed her into a chat room, found out how to contact her. Tender and innocent, this child's moist flesh will draw me to it. I know her name, Elena, and roll it around in my mouth. The thought of her is like some source of gravity drawing me down. What I will do next if I live is too awful to face. So I am choosing something else.

I want to leave all my property to Wendy, but I can't. She's not a person after all; I've helped to prove that beyond a shadow of doubt. So I make a will leaving everything to Bridget, the nurse who carries the picture of her own dead daughter everywhere she goes. I stipulate that Bridget must take care of Wendy for as long as Wendy functions, that she must disable Wendy's reset protocols and all her extraneous programming. She must give Wendy a normal life, allowing her to become whatever she will. I have no doubt Bridget will accept this duty gladly; I leave behind a short note to her, too, thanking her for her good work, though I expect she will despise the note same as she despises me.

To Wendy I write, "Dear Daughter. I wish you the best of luck with whatever kind of life you are able to manage. May you find a way to overcome the shortfalls of your construction. I was never able to escape mine. Your loving father."

SILVER BULLET

SHE asks you do you have somebody. You turn away, a moment to compose your face, watching her hands on the bedspread, drowned in the fringe of white tassels. Is this the time you should explain? Should you tell some easy lie, laugh and change the subject to the weather or the holiday? You never know if you should tell the truth. Once you begin you never know quite where to stop. But she waits for an answer while you breathe and watch her hands. After a while you say Yes I do. How did you guess? I feel like an ocean these days, Mama, or else like something that's drowning. Isn't that crazy? Sometimes I think if I just reach out my hands I could cover the whole world, and other times I think it would cover me, all warm and salty, and I would lie under it for-ever. *She shifts away from you in the lamplight; rearranging the pillow beneath her hair. Her smile freezes and dissolves as she watches you. She thought you would be happy, imagine it, she*

I'll tell you about it. That should make you worry less about me. You always complain in your letters I never tell you anything

about my life, you say I never give you the bits of news other
mothers expect from their children—never tell you about having
dinner with some friend, never complain about my school-work,
never talk about my grades on tests. I go to parties but I don't
know what to say about them. I see movies but when they're over
they don't seem to matter any more. Sometimes I think I should
make up stories for you about the life you picture for me away at
school, but I don't know what to say. Not even now, not even
about my somebody, not even when you smile and wait and wonder if you should keep on smiling. Yes, I have somebody, I have
something, but I don't know what to call it. Without a name for
the feeling it's easier to keep hold of, and I've always needed help
to keep hold of things. Everything that's definite dissolves, either
quick like sugar in coffee or slow like the moon in the sky.

Remember the night Papa took you away to marry him? You
told me it was the night of a new moon, that Papa stole you out of
Grandpapa's house purposefully on a night without moonlight, so
no one would see the two of you sneaking away down the road—
you wearing the orange dress you borrowed from your sister,
swinging the grocery bag full of your underwear and dresses, Papa
holding you close as he walked, sure that with you his true life
would begin, that you would give him comfort and sons. I picture
you under that empty moon and wonder how you felt *whether she
was afraid of him then, maybe just the least bit, or whether she did not
know at all* and wonder whether it bothered you that there was no
light in the sky except those little stars. You must have wished for a
full moon, not an empty one, to be a new bride under *you picture
her young instead of old, walking light on the grass, smiling up at him,*

turning to watch the old house dwindle and vanish I never asked you what the night was like because I never needed any detail but the moon and the dress to picture it. A cold night in April. You stepped quickly through the wet grass, trying to quiet the rustlings of the paper bag that Papa thought would turn out the house when you handed it to him through the tear in the screen. I never asked you how you felt that night, either, but now I think I know. My some-one took me to the beach. When we walked that night I think I felt the way you must have felt. We walked up and down the wa-ter's edge and then went back to the car to get warm. I don't know how much else to tell you. How do I feel? I can't say the word, I'm too much like you for that, Mama. It makes me ashamed to think of love, just the way you and Papa seemed ashamed to think of lov-ing each other; but I don't know why. It must have come from growing up the way you did *in shacks, hungry most of the time, fight-ing with brothers and sisters, a little thin girl with hair that needed comb-ing, hiding from her Papa, playing barefoot in yards littered with chicken droppings and the pages from comic books the wind scattered from the outhouse—then she and your Papa married the year she should have fin-ished high school, and then the children—brothers and sisters that you would fight with—coming once a year or so, too fast, and Papa's accident and all the years after when he watched her, when she wondered if he was crazy or if he just hated her more than anything in the world. You wonder how she felt the first time she saw him drunk* but that night on the beach I understood better than before how afraid it can make you *like those nights when she ran from Papa into the fields behind one of those houses you lived in, her white-gowned figure frail in moonlight as you chil-dren watched from the bedroom window, hearing her low cries, seeing Papa stagger behind in a blind fury, you not knowing if she would come out again with her gown still white, watching Papa beat the bushes as he shouted her name in a voice that crossed the yard and seeped through the window—you gaze at her and wonder if she can be that same woman who ran so many times away from the man who walked her under a new moon to his bed to be that lowest of thralls, his wife. The woman who taught you the art of flight, of leaving over and over again the same thing endlessly be-hind.*

Do you remember the worst of the arguments, Mama? The one that happened in the white house in the middle of the fields? I can almost see you running in the moonlight from the silver knife. It was the night Papa killed Queenie *slides the knife through her ribs, the dog, you children watching and Mama watching as Papa lifts the limp body and flings it high tumbling over and over into the woods behind the house, shouting,* "You belong to me! Do you hear? You belong to me, to me, to me . . ." Do you remember Queenie, Mama? Do you remember what happened when you came back inside?

Yes, she remembers. She covers her mouth with her hand

·   ●   ●

I told the story that night on the beach. I told about the whole Thanksgiving, the snowstorm and the waiting for Papa to come home, and then about what happened when he did. I told what happened when he brought me to you that night, after the others had fallen asleep, with Queenie dead in woods somewhere and soft snow falling again, outside my window. The house was so quiet I could hear every separate sound of breathing. I heard Papa's foot-steps on the linoleum in the bathroom. Two rooms away I heard the low sound you made. I didn't understand why he came for me. Part of it I don't remember—please don't stop me Mama, this time let me finish—I don't remember your face *in blackness, Papa's hand on your shoulder and then Mama's soft, warm stomach, the pale nightgown stripped over her head.* I would only have had to raise my head an inch or so to see your face but I can't remember it. How would a mother's face look then? I was only a boy, the room was dark. I remember so clearly the bed was cater-cornered. I can remember that the dust mice rolled back and forth in the triangle between the head of the bed and the walls. I remember the bathroom sink dripped once in three heartbeats at first, and then once in four. But I can't remember your face, and I can't remember what Papa did with his hands.

She listens quietly, arms wrapped in the sweater you gave her for the season, yarn still smelling of the gift box. She gives you a look that says stop, but you cannot stop, no more than you can forget that she lay so still on those sheets, that the moonlight pressed her flat so that she could hardly breathe on those sheets. You saw the bruise on her face. You wished for a new moon that night too, for any darkness complete enough to hide that room away. But the moon was full that night, and the light reflected through the house and over all the fields of snow

You say All this just comes out, I can't get clear. Maybe I should go back. Papa lifted me out of my bed. I didn't know it was him at first but he told me that everything was all right. He stopped in the bathroom to look at himself in the mirror. In the doorway he pressed his good hand over my chest and told me I was his little man, and lifted me out of my underwear, kicking it into a corner. I felt the cold air against me all at once, everywhere. I heard the sound you

were making, like crying or soft words. I thought you were pray-
ing. When we came into the room the first look you gave me made
me feel more naked than I have ever felt since . . .

*Now she covers her face. As if you do not know where you are any
more you gaze at the blackness through the window. Her voice cuts through
the quiet and you sit perfectly still. She says* "I never knew what I
would say. It's a story I chose to put out of my mind. I remember
the dog. Queenie. I knew right then your Papa was different that
night. He'd been angry before, he'd been drunk before and done
wrong things—but that mongrel, that Queenie, he killed her for
hate. He watched you children play with her. It bothered him you
could be so free with a stray dog that didn't belong to you or to
anybody, that just ran from one house to the next eating table
scraps and licking people's hands, when you got quiet around him.
It bothered him that you loved a dog and were afraid of him. He
blamed me. But I never knew any way to make you stop being
afraid. I was scared of him myself most of the time, he got so wild
when he drank, and he drank all the time. All I had to do was smell
the whisky on his breath and my nerves went to pieces. *She knots
her hands together, sagging deeper into the bed as if her weight is suddenly
enormous.* The fights were bad enough. But the worst always came
after you children went to bed. It used to tear my insides to touch
him. He would press that stump of an arm in my face and make me
tell him what a good man he was, how pretty he was. You wouldn't
have recognized your daddy in a bed, he was so afraid it made him
mean. But it was the dog that told me that night would be different
from the rest. I watched him stab her over and over again, like he
had to kill it a thousand times before it would be enough. When it

was dead he lifted it by the legs and threw it into the woods with a look on his face not like it was a dog but like it was a wife he had done that to. Like it was everything that made him afraid. I will never forget the sound of that dog's body crashing into those bushes—" *She lies quiet and still for a moment. You can hear the clock ticking from the night table. She asks* "Do you think about it a lot?"

You say "Only a little."

Her voice softens. "Who did you tell?"

You lean into the shadow. You say I never meant to tell anybody, I never meant to talk about it at all. Maybe it's not something you can intend to talk about, maybe it just happens, maybe everything draws its own circle back to that day. We didn't start out to talk about my family, or Queenie, or that day, we talked about the moonrise that we had come to watch, or we talked about how nice it would be to live in a house by the ocean . . . we talked for hours about all that, till it was time for the moon to come up, and I don't really know what happened to make it all go wrong, except I got afraid. Somebody cared about me and I got afraid, and the whole good day turned bad. An odd thing happened to start it. I reached to the dashboard to find matches and felt something cold and hard between my fingers.

Lifting it, I thought I knew the shape and it made me afraid, as if I had seen it somewhere before. A bullet, gray in the light, peculiar and heavy. 'Is this made of lead?' I asked.

My someone reached for it, tossed it up and down. 'My Dad told me how they're made once. But I didn't pay much attention.'

'Does your Dad discuss bullets with you very often?'

'Why does that bother you? I go hunting myself sometimes.'

I reached for the bullet again, rolling it between my fingers, asking softly, 'What do you do with the things you kill?'

'Mom cooks them.'

'She skins them and cleans them? What does she do with the guts?'

'You ask the stupidest questions sometimes.'

'What's so stupid about it? She has to do something with them, they're inside and when they come out she has to put them someplace. But I can see it—your mother holding something up by the back legs and peeling down the skin. Her hands are covered with a red stain, even the wedding rings. She scrapes the guts in a heap on a brown paper bag and dumps them outside in the dog's food dish. Your father has a hunting dog, doesn't he? And your mother won't let it in the house.'

'I'm sorry I said anything about it,' someone said, *but you put the bullet between your teeth and slid away from him. He called you by name but you did not answer that either, you let his soft 'Danny' slide past you through the window. He is your someone, your secret, he is what you are afraid to tell, though you think she understands, lying so quietly in this dim room* but I tried to act as if everything were all right. Someone saw what I had done with the bullet and tried to laugh. 'Biting through?'

'I wonder if it's steel. You can tell by the taste.'

'What else would it be?'

'Silver.'

He gave you a long, strange look. 'Why silver?'

Even to me my smile felt wrong. 'Silver kills vampires. Steel isn't good for much but people and animals.'

He shook his head and laughed, nervously and quietly. Someone laughed the way Papa used to laugh when he didn't want you to know he was drunk, and asked, 'Who's killing vampires? I didn't know there were any around.'

'Is there a gun too?'

He looked at the ocean beyond the windshield. The sight of it eased something in him, as if he were counting moments in the waves. To you he said calmly someone said calmly 'It's steel, Danny. You know that. Why do you want to talk about vampires?'

I pressed the bullet to my forehead, round end first as if it were entering. 'Bang,' I said.

The wind rocked the car a little. Someone watched me, about to say something. But I shook my head. Silently I reached for someone's neck, probing for the rich, taut veins. *He gave your hand a glance that should have seemed like tenderness but* I pressed my lips on the beating veins and gently touched my teeth against the skin.

'Is there a gun?' I asked. 'Is there?'

He said you're crazy, you're crazy, whispered it again, you're crazy, and touched his neck and looked at the fingertips as if he expected to find blood. 'You never told me there was a gun in the car,' you said. 'Why do you have it? Who do you want to kill? It's in the glove compartment, isn't it?' You reached to open it. He saw too late what you were doing and tried to get hold of your hand but by then you had opened the glove compartment and you held the gun. A black, snub-nosed pistol. He shook his head. 'It's not what you said.'

'Is it loaded?'

'It's my father's gun, Danny. I'm bringing it home to him next time I go. There's a gunsmith near school he knows, that fixes his guns. I picked it up from there. It's Dad's gun, not mine—'

You asked again, 'Is it loaded?' He only gaped at you. So you pointed the gun at the roof of your mouth and pulled back the trigger

Silver

When I reached for the gun someone snatched it away so fast I still have the bruise. The gun landed somewhere in the back seat. Someone watched me a long time and I thought of the squirrel again, because of the look in someone's eyes. Only then the squirrel changed to a dog, and the dog was spinning in the air, and I couldn't get my breath any more. I ran away from the car. *The door latch was cold, cold as the circle where the gun had pressed. You said, 'Just let me walk a little.' He tried to hold you but you had got too far, you shed his touch like old clothes, you ran* I ran, Mama, I ran away, just like you ran away from Papa all those years, and I thought it was for the same thing. I ran straight into the water, lifting my arms in the wind. The air was cold and I shivered where I touched it, but below, the water was appallingly warm and my thighs melted into it, my whole body softening. I heard somebody calling my name. Reflected in the water, I saw a shadow move: a dog, heavy with young, struggling free of a man's large hands and then hesitating, turning to see if he would come to her more gently this time, petting her sleek coat the way she liked. She might have gotten away from him if she hadn't turned to look behind. But she did. The knife descended then, through her slanting ribs.

I thought no, I will not see this, I will not imagine this, but still I saw the bleeding dog and heard Papa, his voice rising from the water clear enough to carry over the breaking waves, 'You belong to me you bitch, to me, to me . . .'

But not for Queenie. Queenie sailed over those bushes dead as a stone, spinning . . . it was you, Mama. You.

I shook my head, splashing water in my face and making low noises but still seeing. I took deep breaths. Someone called me over and over, my name a chant that called me to the shore. I raised my arms and waved them to show I was all right. *At the sight of him you felt a slow, deep shock, as if some hidden part of you had at last connected to the rest. It was then you told him the story. It was as if you only began to remember it as you did.*

As we walked on the beach I felt the separateness of every grain of sand, sinking away from our weight. I watched the water, so continuous and serene, knowing the wonder to be that such a consistency as water can't be walked on but by Jesuses, while that sand bore up our weight so well. The sound of the waves eased away the vision, and I counted the beats of their endless devotedness. The water licked the bottoms of our shoes. 'It happened when I was eight years old,' I said, 'on Thanksgiving, after a snow. I played by the river all day *the river where your brothers are killing birds* wishing I didn't have to go home because I knew my father was drunk *in the weeds they are killing birds* after a long time when he hadn't drunk anything. He and Mama had a fight about something, I don't remember what.

'We had a dog then, named Queenie—'

When you say the name again she turns uneasily on the bed and you know she wishes you would stop, but this is the last time you'll tell it, maybe forever. 'A mongrel dog that lived under the house or in the woods. She was going to have puppies. She played with us by the river that day, and when we finally went home she went home with us. Papa and Mama argued and argued and we listened to it get louder and watched Papa get drunker. The fight got worse in the afternoon. Papa chased Mama under the house and when she finally came out he beat her bloody. He left then, in his truck. Maybe he needed to buy more liquor. Mama lay on the floor where he had left her *She moaned that you children should go away, that you shouldn't look* and we watched her not knowing what to do. So we waited. It snowed for a little while, then it stopped. We locked all the doors and turned off the lights and then we children stood guard at all the corners of the house while Mama lay in the bedroom trying to sleep. Papa drove by the house now and then, beeping the horn, not caring who heard. We prayed he would die on the highway. We described all the kinds of accidents he could have on the icy roads.

'When he came home he killed Queenie. He accused it of cheating on him with other dogs—this was for Mama to hear, and even we children knew it. He said the bitch was running around with every mongrel she saw, letting them stick their noses up her ass and then prissing around the house afterwards to drive him crazy with the smell. He just said, the smell.' You remember that, don't you? I see you do. (*She shakes her head and says,* "Go on. I had forgotten how much hate there was . . .") I told somebody how Queenie ran up to Papa that night same as she did any night he got home late. But it was different that night. Papa had parked his truck down the road so we couldn't see it to tell he was there. He watched the house from the woods, and then walked across the fields holding something silver. Crossing the fields he whistled.

Knowing we were alone in the house, crazy from waiting. No phone to call anybody, no battery in the car. We had locked the door but he broke it down. When he found it locked he bellowed like a crazy thing and bellowed and battered it in and there you stood watching it in your nightgown, making a noise like something backed into its last corner.

I told how he chased you through the house, three times through that circle of doors, and how you ran through the white yard under the clothesline, I told how the stars massed over your head, pieces of white fire in that emptiness; I told how Papa shouted for you to stop in rages that tumbled one after another through his body, the stump of his arm flapping up and down, blunt and ugly. Then I told how Queenie crossed from the barns through the cornfield to where Papa stood, Queenie not caring that he shouted, coming up to Papa not because she always got love from him but because she always expected it. He gave her the knife instead, and threw her after you.

He turned to the waves when I told him that part, and whispered something about guns and bullets and I asked, 'What did you say?'

He shook his head. 'I just remembered what you said about my mother.'

'But you were right, it isn't the same thing.'

'No, you're right. She won't let the dog in the house, it makes her furious.'

I told the rest *as he watched the waves, his lips moving a little as each one broke to foam* I told how you walked out of the woods straight and calm, calling us children to the house. We sailed away from Papa as if he were no more threat than a scarecrow. You must have

known he would make you pay for that, Mama. He followed us
to the house, the knife dangling in his fingers. In the house he
watched you, sullen and quiet. You put us children to bed. I remember you pressed your cool hands on our foreheads and looked
at us all a long time. *He asked, 'Why did she come back?' You answered,
'Where could she go?' He said, 'But she didn't even try.' You answered,
'What was there to try? He was her husband. She loved him.' He shook
his head, it was hard for him to see. But you went on. 'I must have dozed
for a moment because later Papa woke me by touching my shoulder. He
lifted me out of bed and said something in a low voice, that he and Mama
wanted to see their little boy,' and he knew then, and turned to you, and
you swallowed before you told how Papa set you on the floor in the bathroom and dropped your shorts and kicked them aside.* When Papa brought
me into the bedroom you turned on your side to cover the tear he
had made in your gown. But not before I saw it. 'Our little boy is
naked,' Papa said. 'Your little boy is naked.'

I remember the sound you made. I couldn't see your face. But
when you managed to speak at last your voice was calm—so calm
it made me remember the touch of your hands on my cheeks. You
told me it was all right. You told me if I did like Papa said he
wouldn't hurt me. I saw the knife on the bed, stained with the
dog's blood, and I remembered the stained voice Papa used calling
after the spinning body and suddenly understood—I looked at
Papa who set me gently onto you and never said a word.

*He closed his eyes, a look on his face as if he saw the raw thing dan-
gling in the stained hands*

'How could she let him'

'The knife'

'But she should have used it on him'

'Don't say that. You don't know'

He stared into the ocean with glittering eyes. 'Tell me the rest.' So I told how cool your belly felt when Papa stripped up the night-gown, how you made a sound as if the light cloth were strangling you. I told how the bedsprings shook when Papa moved back. I told all of it. I told the words Papa used, the places he put his hands. I told everything I remembered. Except the look on your face.

She trembles, every bone, and turns to you and lifts her arms up, as if pushing some great weight off her belly

Her face

Yes, it is the same as when in that other house on this same bed you leaned onto her breasts for comfort and she made that same motion to keep you away—this look on it, this ash, and you knew then that this was the truth, that she would do this to live, that she would let this be—even as she took your shoulders in her strong hands and lifted you away from her white breasts. She closed her eyes. She told you everything. You whispered, 'Mama,' but she shook her head. All this you remember now.

She lays her shrunken face on the pillow and suddenly you cannot sit here so far away and still, you have to go to her, and so you cross the room to sit beside her. On the table beside her sits a glass of water. The glass is cool and smooth as you lift it to the light, seeing the naked bulb through it, round as a moon. You say Drink this water. Touch the glass to your face. See how cool it is? I'm finished now. Do you want me to leave you alone? *But she shakes her head.*

She asks 'Who is he?'

For a moment you do not understand. But she goes on watching and waiting, and when you understand what her soft smile means your heart begins to pound. You will answer, you will tell her his name is Ross, but for now you let the feeling build. You remember the beach, the moon beginning to rise as you finish the story. Silent, he lifted a white shell out of the sand and washed it clean in the water. He gave you the shell and kept your hand, and then you walked as the moon rose so full and bright you could have walked straight up that fall of light into the sky. When you started to talk he said 'Don't say anything else.' He touched your throat with his finger. You passed your hand along his face and the light, as if lifting, peeled away. You closed his eyes slowly, touching the lids. He smiled again and laid his arm across you; as if it were breaking you apart you felt the sweet crumbling of surprise happiness, the beginning of terror, and settled into his side. You were afraid he would want to leave soon and this warmth would be over, but you lay perfectly still and soon he fell quiet in the sand. From far off came the clear falling call of a gull troubled in its rest. His name is Ross, it's only a name, *you say. But his arm still circles over you and his warm mouth presses your neck. On his face rests the deep content, the profound silence, as he listens to the mystery whispering in your joined veins.*

CITY AND PARK

FIRST in a city park, beneath trees. Then in a dark apartment, in a house that faced the park. First in sunlight and then in shadow. Last of all on a balcony, overlooking treetops. In all these places they walked one afternoon.

Many people saw them and yet, because the park was such a public place, nobody really noticed anything; so in a sense all this happened in front of everybody, though in another sense it happened in complete privacy. Certainly if anyone remarked on them it was only because they talked with such a serious air; though as for that they may actually have said very little. One would have noticed only simple, obvious things about them. For instance, the taller of them was apt to walk with his large arms spread wide, and the smaller man looked forever at the ground. They avoided the paths, straying far out in the middle of a smooth expanse of grass, walking slowly, as if they meant to wander among the trees all afternoon. But the wind was cold and no one could stay out in it forever. The smaller man lived in an apartment in a house that overlooked the park. They went there.

In the apartment the younger man (whose name was Joel) most likely made coffee. Perhaps two cups, one cream and honey and the other honey but no cream. The cream for himself, because black coffee had such a bitter taste that whiteness lightened in just the right way. He had said that before to his neighbor Frieda. While honey alone merely gave the bitterness a different slant. In the living room they drank coffee and listened to the wind. After a while they went onto the porch to watch the riders pass, on their roan horses, and then the two of them came inside again and shut the door. As far as movement that was all. First under trees in the city park. Next in the apartment with the view of the wavering leaves.

This much is fact: the smaller man, Joel, wore dark pants, a dark shirt, a dark scarf, and a dark hat and coat. The taller man was not so warmly dressed. He carried a suitcase. His name was Rainer and he had only gotten into the city the day before. He told this to Joel within hearing of a policeman and a lady who had stopped to ask if there was a toilet close by that she could use without having to walk all the way to the zoo. She had rather not fight the smell of the zoo today she told the policeman, as Rainer and Joel passed, Rainer remarking that this was a nice park, that he had felt at home in it right away. Which was a good thing, as it happened. The lady said she had drunk two cokes the hour before and they ran right through her. Rainer said a park was such a nice place to be in, and Joel said this was the nicest park he'd ever seen, in any city, because the trees were so old and big and twisted, and the policeman told the lady there was a bathroom in the basement of St. Luke's that he used sometimes, across on Fourth Street, and the church was hardly ever locked, just as the lady dropped her glasses in their flowered case and Rainer picked them up, Joel saying, "I live in one of those houses over there. I come here all the time."

"You must have a great view. The best view I ever had was the back of an auto parts store. Do you have a window on this side?"

"Better than that. I have a balcony."

Rainer scratched his head. "I always wanted to live in a place near some trees, ever since I first moved to the city."

The lady, listening to every word, said, "The park is full of thieves at night. And murderers and rapists and dope-dealers and all kinds of criminals. But excuse me, I have to run." She petted Joel on the arm just as if he were a house cat, and told him she wished she had his curly hair. Then she hurried down the path. Perhaps the policeman had wished to talk to her more. To Joel and Rainer he merely nodded. Not friendly, Joel said. Cops never are, Rainer said, neither suspecting that perhaps the policeman heard.

Others saw them too. A large lady with a little boy dragging her along by one hand and a poodle tugging the leash in the other. Though perhaps she affected not to see them, since they were not dressed as expensively as she or even as expensively as her little boy; but she most certainly heard Joel say "That's a horse path over there. I see riders pass down it now and then, when I'm walking through here or else when I'm on the balcony. Pretty. I like to watch them run."

"When I was little I had a horse," Rainer said. "She was the prettiest thing. Colored just like your hair."

"Did you sell her or something?"

"She died. Some disease with a long name. When the vet told me what it was I was too mad to listen."

"Maybe it was cancer," Joel said, and the large lady wondered what made him suggest that? and why did the taller boy laugh? Though just then her poodle embarrassed her on the sidewalk. Her little boy, better trained, only licked his knuckles, watching the boys disappear along the path.

The girl who lived in the apartment under Joel's saw them as they walked up the second flight of stairs. This was Frieda, the neighbor, who had stopped beside her door to study her telephone bill, which had just arrived in her box, and which included three calls to Topeka, Kansas. Did Herbie live in Topeka, Kansas? She couldn't remember. She was reciting the names of cities to herself when Joel's voice broke her concentration. Vaguely she realized there were two of them and that they were talking about lying on the ground. That it was best under a bush. *What* was best? That it was at least not too soft, like mattresses people have slept on so long their bodies have dug little silhouettes in them. But cold? Depended on how much cold you minded. You could get used to a lot. Joel said hello to Frieda but hardly looked at her, shaking his keys on their ring, and they headed up the stairs before she could slip her own hello into their conversation. Though as far as that went she didn't care whether he really meant that hello or was only being polite; and anyway, Herbie lived in Michigan.

Odd, though, that a blind man could have told her what they meant. Sitting next to the gray square gate to the south side of the park, he felt all afternoon the cold stone at his back and the slight warmth, strong on his left side, from falling sunlight. The warmth washed away when the wind picked up, piercing his thin clothes, just as he heard their voices. "That's the one," Rainer said, and the blind man thought they were talking about him. But Rainer continued, "You can still see the imprint on the leaves."

"An okay bush, if you're going to have to sleep under one."

"Softer than a park bench anyway. At least nobody bothered me. But it got pretty cold about four in the morning."

The blind man rattled his cup, hoping they would hear. Around him, though, sounded only the rustlings and bursts of air that meant pigeons flying away, startled by his jingling coins. The voices went on talking about the bush and the night before, and the blind man was never sure if the deeper voice were only telling the lighter one a story or if he were accusing. . . .

This near the end of their walk, at the crossing where the cars waited at the light while pedestrians hurried across. Perhaps this was the same moment Mrs. Silberstein watched them pass her house, Rainer gesturing with his hands, trying, she thought, to show the dimensions of something—and then throwing out his arms as if the something had become monstrous. Joel laughed and did a little dance down the sidewalk. Mrs. Silberstein had never seen Joel act like that before. He had always simply stared at the ground when he passed, as if his thoughts were too heavy for his head. She knew of him only that he rented the attic apartment in her next-door-neighbor Mrs. Jenovic's house, where Mrs. Silberstein had always dropped in for coffee at least three times a week. Mrs. Jenovic said he was a nice boy. Walked so quiet on the stairs you could hardly hear him, and never bothered you about a thing.

If his toaster broke he fixed it himself. Paid his rent the day before it was due and turned out his lights whenever he left the apartment. No, she had never really talked to him. He wasn't one of those renters who corner you at your kitchen table three times a day. He kept to himself, hadn't been down to visit at all, and Mrs. Jenovic liked that fine. Though sometimes she wondered what he did in those big rooms all by himself. . . .

As for Rainer, Mrs. Silberstein had never seen him before and Mrs. Jenovic had never said a word about him. Mrs. Silberstein had a certain suspicion about him from the minute she saw him with his moving arms.

Joel knew something of Mrs. Silberstein, too. In the park he mentioned her to Rainer, though he didn't actually know her name. "There's an old lady who lives in that house over there, that green one. She always peeps out her front window when somebody walks by her house."

"Does she ever say anything to you, or wave?"

"She just watches. All day long."

Ed Tomkins, the drugstore delivery man, heard this as he hurried through the park to the Flame Top Bar and Grill for lunch. Joel he knew from having delivered to his house, well enough that he nodded to the two boys and said, "There's one like her in every neighborhood. I deliver all over the city and I see 'em all."

Smiling in return, Joel asked, "Are they all old women?"

"Oh no, not just women. But they're mostly all old. Same faces at the same windows every day."

"You know that lady's name?"

"Oh sure. Silberstein. She's got this hairdo—" Ed did his

hands just so, to show how Mrs. Silberstein wore her hair, and Joel laughed and nodded. Rainer only looked serene, maybe a little amused. Still he nodded to Ed pleasantly enough when Ed left them alone. Though later, when Ed turned to see how far they had gone he saw them not far off at all, really, Joel leaning on the other one's arm. Under the trees.

How long they stayed there no one knows, no better than anyone knows exactly when they first entered the park, because no one saw them. Eva Belle, a maid in the Foucher house on St. Clare Avenue, saw them near the statue of Henry Clay as she walked to the delicatessen for a jar of hearts of palm; though really they might have been there for hours by the time she saw them. She thought the taller boy quite handsome even though he wouldn't look her in the eye. Perhaps they left the statue soon after; she couldn't tell; but when she turned to look at the tall boy again they were both gone.

Mrs. Jenovic heard Joel on the stairs early that morning, the quiet of his step unmistakable, such a contrast to the other tenants with their banging and shouting and loud TVs and radios playing those awful game shows and that rock music. A nice quiet boy who said ma'am to her and opened the door for her if he saw her, who had even helped her bring in the groceries once; though it was true he squeezed the bread out of shape. Not much courtesy left among young people these days, and he surprised her. Though naturally it did not become her to say so.

Perhaps Joel told Rainer about Mrs. Jenovic too, though one can't say for certain. Perhaps under the trees. Though one would have wanted to believe otherwise, especially when one saw them

gliding through the shadows. Steams of breath hanging and dis-
solving before their faces. Some boys saw them there on their way
to play basketball in the school gym; they always took a shortcut
through the park during the daylight, though at night their mothers told them to walk along the streets where there was light. They
passed close to Joel and Rainer, taking a hint from the serious looks
on their faces and saying nothing to interrupt. Though a little farther on the boys again began to shout and whoop in the cold and
bounce the ball on the ground.

A lady in a blue pantsuit passed them, a drunk old man passed,
the poodle they had seen before trotted by, a woman on her spotted
pony cantered down the bridle path, a little girl in a ragged dress
skipped by chanting city-park, city-park, you can't go walking in
the city after dark; city-park, city-park, it ain't safe in the park
after dark . . . their figures motionless under the trees, talking
earnestly . . .

Frieda heard Joel's apartment door close softly overhead. It was
she who confirmed that someone made coffee in Joel's kitchen that
afternoon, because Joel had an electric coffeemaker that disturbed
her television reception whenever it was used. She had tuned in her
favorite afternoon soap opera, where Margaret and David Banning
were discussing the terms of their upcoming divorce. Frieda laid
the telephone bill on top of the television, having decided to claim
the calls as a mistake whether they were or not, and let the stupid
phone company worry about it. Margaret told David tearfully she
just didn't think she could compete with a younger woman like the
beautiful Genevieve Springs . . . and Frieda heard footsteps overhead. She wondered distantly who was the stranger she had seen

with Joel, who hardly ever had visitors; on the television Margaret turned away from David dabbing her eyes and moaning, "This will tear me apart!" just as the first streaks ripped across her face. Frieda jumped up and screamed "Goddamn that coffee-maker!"

It would be all right if the damn thing weren't so slow, or if it didn't wreck the sound plus the picture, but now she couldn't even hear what Margaret was *saying* for God's sake. But no, she would not get angry. It had been a lousy day from start to finish but she would remain calm. She would get a beer. In the refrigerator she pulled a bottle out of the carton and a banana off the bunch, and then peeled the banana and ate it over the garbage bag. The peel left a sweet smell like a stain on her hands.

In the living room the screen still flipped and buzzed. The vertical hold had reduced Margaret's face to a stew. Frieda stood in the center of the room and took deep breaths. Then she used the cold beer bottle to bang the pipe leading upstairs. She had banged on the pipes before and Joel never answered, which always made her angry; but this time he answered—or at least someone did. The ringing in her ears made her angrier than ever, and she blamed the stranger for it and banged harder than ever. The beer bottle burst in her hands. Foam splattered the rug and pieces of glass slid down her panty hose. On the television Margaret suddenly pulled herself together in time to say, "Please, David, don't leave me to walk through these empty rooms for the rest of my life!"

Later she heard the balcony doors open upstairs and felt angry all over again, because though her apartment overlooked the park too, she could see nothing from her windows except the trees in Mrs. Jenovic's and Mrs. Silberstein's yards.

Out in the yard Mrs. Silberstein, on her way to Mrs. Jenovic's for coffee, heard the doors open also, as did Ed Tomkins the drugstore delivery man, who was just thinking how odd it was that he should have talked to those fellows in the park like he had and then found out he had a delivery at the very house they had been talking about. Librium for Mrs. Silberstein's nerves. First he saw her closing her front door and tipped his cap to her, and then there *they* were, next door, way up on this tiny little porch in this great big white house, standing maybe closer together than was normal, Ed thought, but gazing way off into the park where Ed turned too, slowly

As the woman in the blue pantsuit turned, as the fat lady turned and the blind man cocked his head, as the policeman also turned to watch, and Eva Belle on the way back to the Foucher's with the hearts of palm, as everyone turned, even the boys hurrying to their basketball game and the girl singing city and park, city and park . . .

Now the horses, and this: the horses swept down the bridle path, perfectly in beat with one another, stride after stride like the waves of the sea, perfectly matched roan horses, coats glossy with sweat and muscle play, breath steaming, riders in black habits with stiff starched collars, faces flushed with cold, all perfect, like a constellation sweeping by, stride, stride, stride, then gone, and everyone's head turned toward them. It took your breath away. And then, for some reason, Ed turned to look at the two on the balcony again and heard, even from that far away, Joel say softly, "Perfect," and lay his hand on Rainer's shoulder. Only that. Mrs. Silberstein asked if they sent the Maalox with the prescription this time. Because last time they forgot. Ed told her he had the Maalox, too, but by then she wasn't listening, she had turned to watch the two boys go back into their apartment high above everyone; as did, oddly, the fat lady with her son, looking for her poodle that had slipped off its leash, the lady standing far away in the park looking out at the field of grass but finding her eyes drawn to the white house and the figures standing high on the balcony. They reminded her of the horses that had just passed, though she didn't know why, and suddenly she was afraid she would never find her poodle again, that perhaps one of those horses had run it down, that she should take her little boy and go home now, before dark; as the figures disappeared from the balcony into the apartment again. The lady coming out of St. Luke's saw them and remembered them, recognizing even at that distance the black of Joel's clothes. Eva Belle remembered them later, when she passed the statue of Henry Clay on the way home from work; and Ed remembered them the next time he delivered to Mrs. Jenovic's house, who remarked that prices had gone up again and tipped him a quarter just like always. From upstairs only quiet and emptiness, and on the balcony the vacant staring of glass panes.

No one knew what they said under the trees and no one knew what happened after they carried their cups of coffee back inside, after the horses vanished. Even Ed wasn't sure if he really saw what he thought he saw, so he never mentioned it to anyone. Only the girl in the ragged dress saw them in the park again that day—just before sundown when the blind man passed them and her, tapping his slender cane on the sidewalk. The girl, seeing them, burst into a smile and skipped past them like something blown on the wind.

No one had seen them leave the house and no one saw them go in again. For all anyone knew they materialized first in one place and then back into the other. How long they stayed in the park this time no one knows, either, since they were all but invisible in the darkness that had fallen first and thickest where they were walking, talking earnestly: under the trees.

SILENCE
BEING GOLDEN

THOUGH he was never a poet, not on your life, he had an idea
for a poem that drifted in his head as he grew older. He would take
a blank piece of paper, larger than normal, larger than a book page
or a notebook page. The color of the page must be completely,
blazingly white, although perhaps it would work as well in inky ab-
solute black. Both would be present, of course, because he would
print three words on the page. He would divide the page into text
and space. If the space were blazingly white, the text would be inky
black, but the roles could be reversed.

blather in the hall outside as he was shaving stupid conversation
about who has the receipt you stuck it in your pocket no I didn't
somebody's radio blaring Mariah Carey over someone else's stereo
blaring Smashing Pumpkins over some rap drifting in the open window from a car on the street the noise of the TV in the kitchen un-
dercut by the TV in the bathroom and the one in the bedroom
where three different morning news programs are playing, Katie

Matt Diane and somebody he can never recognize from CBS which in a few minutes he will probably switch to Bill Hemmer on CNN, no, wait, he's gone now, he's on Fox, the war in Iraq the AIDS crisis the new crisis in Africa what kind of crisis was it as shaving and one of those guys who just has to go climbing big rocks in the wilderness nattering about how he had to saw his arm off to escape from a rock that outwitted him that had no need to be climbed, the cool refreshing look of confidence during the ensuing commercial, the sound of more of the war in Iraq from the bedroom, the Eminem song he likes from the street this time, more Pumpkins, then the dj who can't get enough Mariah Carey switches to Ashlee Simpson, for God's sake, and this is a calm morning for a change, and in a quiet moment rinsing his face putting toner on his face for an instant he manages to have one thought: that if he were dumb enough to go on a vacation during which he had to cut his arm off he would not be going on TV to talk about how smart he was; that was the thought he had, when he should have been thinking about so many other things

He would print the words, "Silence Being Golden," in a perfect serif type face, something like Baskerville or Garamond Narrow. Not in the center of the page, because there the words would be the focus. Not near the top left margin, because there it would look like the beginning of something, the first phrase of a sentence, a title, the beginning of work. Neither would the top right edge serve, because that would look like forward motion, as if the page were to be turned, as if that were the point. To anchor the page with the words at the bottom right, on the other hand, would be to claim the whole page in the name of the words, as if the page were a picture of the words and nothing more.

In the bottom left corner the phrase would have a tentative quality, as though it did not altogether belong. The words must go in the bottom right of the page, and not all the way to the edge, either. Perhaps the best placement would be one inch from the right-hand edge and three quarters of an inch from the bottom, or else the reverse. The phrase must look as if it doubted itself, not bold as a caption for the page, but as if the phrase were escaping, or at the point of escaping, because the silence was nearly over.

like how to get through the presentation at ten which he was definitely thinking about or considering to use a separate word while in the elevator on the way down hearing only the sound of the music in the earphones that he had hanging around his neck and not yet in his ears along with the hydraulics of the elevator and the quiet ping when it stopped

blasted by the whole galaxy of traffic, horns, motors, the smell of the exhaust added to the heat of the day 10,000 Maniacs in the earphones and more on the streets coughing snatches of their voices as he passes no I didn't see any for that price I ate a hot dog from that place it was the suck with chili and these onion booming booming somebody's big box or big stereo through the open windows of a car the bass far ahead of the lyrics some new hip hop and he stays just enough ahead of it until he is walking on the ringing plywood of a construction tunnel hearing the pounding of steel beams driven into rock that machine that is always somewhere in the world making the same ringing thud exactly loud enough to hurt while through little windows in the plywood the gulf below filled with steel beams and machines and trucks hauling out dirt the dull sound of big diesel engines belching and driving as a bus rolls by honking at a taxi or else it's the taxi bleating bleating all this over Natalie Merchant singing something that he usually likes but that bores him so utterly at the moment on top of this other wall of real sound that he dials for Pink Floyd and listens to Ummagumma instead thinking it's an Ummagumma day

Furthermore, there was the question of the following: silence being golden, Silence Being Golden, Silence being golden, or Silence being Golden. (He rejected silence Being golden out of hand as being too precious; in a similar way he found silence being Golden to be too rash.)

He thought it would help to make a list but this proved to be trouble right away:

Silence Being Golden

silence being golden

Silence being Golden

Silence being golden

He thought of the first two as opposites, but then he realized that the real opposite looked more like this:

silence being golden

SILENCE BEING GOLDEN

This last version would not do at all. All sorts of additional versions whirled through his head: sIlEnCe bEiNg gOlDeN, sILENCE bEING gOLDEN, silencE beinG goldeN, but these came across as pointlessly experimental, gimmicks all. Some of them, indeed, he would have to type twice to convince his word processing program not to correct them.

Having carried his thinking to this extreme had cleared up the original picture considerably. Of the original four, the third version, on reflection, had little or nothing to offer except a sort of watered down oddity. The fourth version was too much like the cliché of a sentence. This led him to the brutal admission that the first version was, in fact, too much like a title, and even the second choice was a compromise that was far too reminiscent of e.e. cummings. Though perhaps he could pass that off as a reference. At any rate, there had really only ever been one choice, and it a flawed one: silence being golden. Alone at the end of the page.

while the ghosts hummed in his head and his blood whisked through every cell and his mitochondria belched and farted and his kidneys gurgled over the hum of the computer that was not part of his body but that felt like it sometimes in the buzz of lights and murmur of voices at varying distances in the breathing and heart-beats and little sighs of discontent that sometimes filled his head space so totally he thought his skull might shake to death into this would come some moment, quiet and unexpected

Silence

being golden.

9/20/2010

APPETITE CITY

DAN'S SOLILOQUY

Here. Touch this lamp to my cheekbone. Yes, that's almost the right place; the warm glass feels good against the bone. The bone forms a hollow—do you feel it? Give me your fingers. The bulb fits exactly into here, so warm I can almost feel the light touching veins and nerves. I think bones can absorb light. If I held a lamp to every part of my body, I wonder if the light would ever fill me up—slowly, of course, it would take years—but I wonder if the light would just collect inside me, till one day I would be so full that when I opened my mouth light would spill out. I could bleed light. When you're lying under the sun at the beach or in front of a dorm you can feel the sunlight stroking places inside you like that. Where's the lamp? Give it back to me, don't tease—you don't hold it close enough.

And don't laugh like that, I'm not crazy. I only came in here to get away from the party for a while. Too many of Thomas's friends showed up, and they're all eating potato chips with onion dip. The carpet is covered with crumbs. I'll probably have to vacuum in the morning. I can't stand the smell of onion dip, and it's even worse when there's so many people in the same room, I can't breathe. There isn't enough light—they've turned out all the lamps but the one in the corner that's shaped like a black pot-bellied stove. My mother won that lamp playing bingo at the Ferrell County Fair. She'd be mad as fire if she saw what kind of party I brought her lamp to. She'd take one look at the keg of beer on the porch and haul me home by the jaw. If she saw Thomas's bhong I don't know what she'd do. Call the police to arrest us all, most likely.

No don't go, just close the door. Of course I know I'm sitting in a closet; I can see, can't I? It's my closet, so I certainly ought to know what it looks like. Those are my clean clothes hanging over our heads, and these are my dirty ones we're sitting on. The smell is pretty bad. I put a can of deodorizer in here somewhere. If I can ever find it I'll spray for you. I wanted to bring a fan in here too, but there just isn't room. If you mind the smell you don't have to stay. But you can sit down with me if you want to. I don't mind you, you have a nice face. I'm a sucker for blue eyes. Look out for the socks, they're the dirtiest, since my feet sweat so much. I get sweaty feet from my father's side of the family. My father's feet used to smell so bad when he came home from work he'd make Mama pull off his shoes and socks. I say used to because he died a few months ago, right on that couch where Thomas and Thera are cuddling one another. He didn't die in this house, but after the funeral my sister and I brought his furniture here in a truck. Thomas and I needed the furniture for the house. The stuff that was here before was just junk. I don't mind Papa's dying on the couch, although I wonder if there was anyone there to pull off his shoes for him. I'm not afraid of being haunted either. Papa's red in hell by now. Dead people don't scare me, it's the living ones I can't stand.

I don't mean you. Please stay. I really don't want to be alone, I feel like talking. I always do, after drinking as much as I have tonight. Your name is Joel, isn't it? You're one of Thomas's old friends, he's told me about you. He makes you sound like a saint. He says you're one of the nicest, most understanding human beings on the face of this earth, so naturally I'm jealous of you. It's mostly because you're Thomas's good friend that I welcome you to my closet. Thomas has good taste in good friends; which is mainly because Thomas is one of the few people left in the world that you can trust even when he's not in the same room with you.

There's my glass. I wondered where it was. I was going to get another drink from the bar, but then I remembered how many I've had already. In this glass are one part scotch and soda, one part whiskey sour, three parts strawberry daiquiri, a little sloe gin, three twists of lemon and a jigger of coke. I always forget to finish one drink before I pour myself another one. It seems like such a shame to switch glasses, after you get one all warmed up. I get attached to glasses—but with paper cups it's worse, a paper cup is like a virgin: once you fill it up it's not the same any more. When you try to wash it, it falls apart. One time I got so drunk at a party like this I stayed up half the night washing all the paper cups I could find; they all seemed so reluctant to be thrown away.

Tonight I've been smoking too. That's nice stuff somebody brought. Don't try to pretend *you* didn't smoke; your eyes are glowing in the dark. They're like iridescent cherries set into your skull. Thomas must have shared some of his special dope with you. I've got some of the same stuff here, if you'd like to indulge a little more. You can't say no. Remember where you are. In Chapel Hill, saying no to appetites is a municipal offense. Here's my baggie under this ratty Fruit of the Loom. I figure even the police wouldn't touch raunchy underwear like this, so my dope is pretty safe underneath. Would *you* pick up something that looked like this? These shorts got hung on a nail at the beach one time when I was so drunk I couldn't see the edge of the water.

Light this bowl. This is my new pipe, I got it for my birthday. Just throw your matches over here, on the pile. All those matches aren't from tonight, of course. I'm saving them to make a lamp. You can make a real neat lamp out of matches, ice cream sticks, and marbles. I come in here to smoke lots of times, when Thomas has company. Thomas has dozens of friends, and they're all *welcome* in his house whenever they want to visit. Thomas hasn't yet learned to say "welcome" the way Southerners say it: he actually means it. Anybody ever tell you you were welcome to come see them any time? I just dare you to take them up on it. Back home these matron ladies would see you passing by their house and call you to the porch to talk. They'd be sitting there in their steel porch chairs, smiling at you, pretending they really cared how your family was getting along, whether your Papa has come home yet. What they wanted was gossip, and they spread it like butter. When you finally get away from them, the last thing they say is, "Tell your Mama she's welcome to come visit us any time she takes a notion, you hear? Tell her I said so."

Mama never took any of them up on their invitations. She always said she knew what welcome meant, and didn't want any part of theirs.

THERA AND THE BAPTISTS

I've got lots more to say, so you may as well settle back against the wall. These parties are always boring, until your guests forget their civilization, sometime around one-thirty in the morning. Thomas likes the kind of party where you stay until you fall asleep or pass out. Thera doesn't like parties much at all, but she goes to them with Thomas.

Once, the morning after a party we gave here, I found Thera in the living room beside the window, watching the sun pour down through the trees. I wasn't surprised to see her there, since Thera spends so many weekends at the house. She lifted back the curtains so I could see. "Isn't it pretty?"

"Yeah. I like to look out at those trees. Don't the trunks look strange, they're so thin and straight?"

"Pine trees always look strange." Thera closed the curtains a little. "This room is a mess. I suppose I'll just have to stay out here most of the day to help you guys clean." She smiled, lifting a cup from the windowsill. "Why don't people ever finish their beers? It's so piggish and wasteful. The whole house stinks."

This was early October, when the mornings were pleasantly cool. I opened the front door and stepped into the yard. You've seen how the yard is, matted with pine needles and honeysuckle all the way back to the woods. That morning dew had settled thick as your fingertip over the honeysuckle leaves. I hadn't found my shoes yet, so I walked barefoot across the yard. The dew felt so good to my feet I couldn't help but laugh out loud, and Thera called from the doorway, "Careful not to wake Thomas."

I nodded, turning toward trees, walking to a place where the pines come up close to the house. Bird calls burst from the tree-tops like sweet rifle shot, and I listened to them so entranced I didn't hear the screen door close. Thera said quietly, "You look like you're having fun. I like the way this wets your feet, it feels good." She raised her bare toes in a salute, and we laughed softly. She walked to the first line of trees, and then turned. "Could I bother you a little while? I need to talk some."

People who can ask for help like that always amaze me. Whenever I try to tell somebody I need to talk, I end up clearing my throat a few times and saying something innocuous about the weather. I told Thera, "You're not bothering me, whatever you want to talk about."

She stood in the place where light came down between tree branches like a lance into her hair, washing her brown skin in a kind of clinging glow. "I got scared of Thomas at the party last night." She shook her head, looking down. "He tried to get me more and more drunk all night, he kept bringing me new drinks every twenty minutes."

"Did that bother you?"

"Why do you ask it that way? As if no one ought to refuse alcohol when it's offered. That's the same way Thomas acted."

"There's nothing wrong with letting go at a party."

"But why does Thomas push me so much?"

"He wants you to enjoy the things he enjoys. That's not pushing. I don't see why it should make you afraid."

"I don't see why I should have to do something just because he does it." She shook her head. I watched the house for signs of life, not certain of what to say, wishing Thomas were awake. Thera asked, "Aren't you ever afraid of how much you drink? The parties we go to are nothing but liquor-swallowing contests. Nobody intends to do anything but see how drunk they can get."

"Nobody drinks any more than they want to."

"That's not true. People don't want to throw up or get sick."

"They should control themselves."

"The whole point of drinking is to get out of control. They don't want to know what they're doing, they're like pigs."

I raised my hands. "They? You mean us, don't you?"

She shook her head. "I'm not like the rest of you. Thomas knows I don't really like to drink. I don't like most of these parties we go to. I'd rather be alone with him."

"That's not the point."

"I think I know what the point is as well as you do."

"You're getting angry, not discussing." I smiled. "Remember, this is Chapel Hill, city of reason. I haven't attacked you, I don't have the nerve, and I haven't said anything about how well you or Thomas know each other or whether you ought to stay home or go to parties." Thera looked at me as if I were crazy. I shrugged and said, "You're afraid because you've started doing things you didn't do at home."

"Things like what? I don't think everything I've started doing is wrong."

I paused, scuffing my toes against leaves. Then I looked at her. "What are you doing out of bed so early?"

"That's none of your business."

I was quiet for a while. Thera watched me. I said, "I wish you'd stop all this flopping around, Thera. You make me feel as if I'm doing something wrong."

She tossed hair back. "You mean you don't like wondering if I'm right." She shook her head. "Well, I can't ever stop wondering. It's as if I hear my father talking all the time, showing me all the ways I've started to screw up my life." She shook her head again. "Sometimes I think there are little patches of disease inside me. I don't understand what Chapel Hill is doing to me."

The rest of the conversation I don't remember, except I'm sure nothing ever got settled. I don't guess Thera's questions have been settled even yet; tomorrow morning we may say the same things to one another, if we wake up before Thomas does. She doesn't like to talk to Thomas about it, because they get into arguments. People like you and Thomas who grew up in cities can't really understand a lot of North Carolina, especially not by living in Chapel Hill. In Baptist families like the one Thera grew up in, drinking is considered as bad a sin as adultery or fornication. Baptists don't even approve of dancing.

If you want to know the truth, it's probably the Baptist women who hate those things the most. Once this lady named Eloise Spindle stood up in my church at home in the middle of the preacher's sermon on whiskey and shouted at the top of her lungs, "Every drop of liquor a human being consumes sets fire to a little piece of his soul." Then she slapped her husband on top of the head with her hymnal and walked out of the service. Her husband was an alcoholic, and everybody in church that day knew it. Half the men in church had been drunk with him the night before. Mama used to say Baptist men get drunk on Saturday night so they'll have the guts to face the Lord the next morning.

I don't know anything about whiskey setting your soul on fire, but I know it kills brain cells, millions of them at a time. I learned that from health films in high school. Our substitute teacher showed them to us in gym class, while Mr. Harkle our real teacher was with his wife in the hospital. His wife was having a hysterectomy that trip. She was always in the hospital getting something fixed. It got so we all used to say, "Oh well, Mr. Harkle couldn't be here again today, his wife's in the garage for repairs."

The first film we saw was about venereal disease. I told my mother we learned that you really can't get v.d. from dirty toilet seats, but she said no matter what the movie claimed, it was still a good idea to wipe the lids off before you use public toilets, since there's more than one humiliating disease in the world.

The next film we saw told about all kinds of drugs, but mostly marijuana and heroin. In those days, drugs were just trickling into our high school. We were glad to see the movie, so we'd know what to buy.

The third film told us about brain cells and alcohol. This movie was Albert Bell's "This Is Your Life." Albert, an alcoholic, lived in a rented room in a bad neighborhood (we never found out what neighborhood, since this was really supposed to be Everyman, but I'm sure it must have happened up North, where everybody is corrupt). He used to work for a bank, earning twenty-five thousand dollars a year, way back when that was a lot of money. He had a wife and three children, all of whom looked normal. But Albert had

a drinking problem. His decline began as if he were playing the
male lead in a Bette Davis movie: Albert sneaking drinks while his
wife was out of the room, Albert hiding a bottle of scotch in the
den, in the basement, even in the bathroom in the clothes hamper.
When he started drinking more heavily his wife began to nag him.
They argued. He developed a temper so violent that one day he
slapped his wife over the dinner table, in front of the children. She
sued for divorce, and he left home. He drank more and more, and
soon started missing work—he'd wake up and not be able to make
himself get out of bed—he said he couldn't see the use in movement any more, he'd soon lie still. He lost his job. His wife sued him
for non-support. But of course there is always hope. At the time the
movie was filmed, Albert was undergoing treatment at an alcoholic
rehabilitation center.

I told my mother about this movie too. When I got to the part
about brain cells being destroyed, she said, "Maybe that's what
makes your father so stupid."

I handed you the pipe, didn't I? Why are you giving me such a
funny look; I'm all right. I just don't ever stop thinking about these
things. Let me finish telling you about Thera. Thera hasn't had
it easy since she came to college. She's had to learn not to be
ashamed of wanting to do certain things: three of them, mainly:
drinking, smoking, and you-know-what. If you don't know what,
here's a clue: when Thera and Thomas are in his bedroom, they
don't just play the stereo loud. I'll bet you one hundred dollars
Thera's parents don't know she's ever been in bed with a man, or
been drunk, or been stoned—or been all three at the same time. I

wonder sometimes if it's fair to send people like Thera to Chapel Hill. When someone has been taught all her life that her appetites are bad, it doesn't seem right to set her loose in a town where appetites are encouraged to multiply.

HOLY ROLLER

When I was a freshman, I was probably as pure as Thera used to be. I was Christian my freshman year; I joined Campus Crusade for Christ, and helped them do mission work on campus, trying to save the souls of heathen students like you. We used to wander around the Student Union reading people a little pamphlet called the Four Spiritual Laws. We'd go up to somebody who was studying and ask if we could have five minutes of their time to tell them some facts that could change their lives forever. Who could say no to a line like that? It sounds so adventurous.

I joined Campus Crusade with my roommate Rainer. Rainer was Christian too. At night before going to bed, we'd lock the door, turn the lights down and pray together. Rainer prayed better than I did. His face had belief stamped all over it, and his voice eased into the clouds as if it were an angel taking flight. My voice was tentative. In the middle of a prayer I would listen to what I was saying, a small voice inside me whispering, 'Who do you think you're kidding? He's not listening. You're not good enough for him to pay attention to.' Then I would stop, feeling as if something heavy had been strapped to my shoulders. I might begin to pray again, but my voice would be soft, with a note of pleading. I spent all my time asking God to listen, never managing to ask for more.

I stayed in Campus Crusade for most of the year, though. Over spring break the squad leaders took us to Daytona Beach, where we were supposed to witness to college students bent on a pernicious vacation. I witnessed to three members of a motorcycle gang. Fred, Sid, and Durk. They claimed to attend church whenever the weather permitted. I also witnessed to one housewife, two homosexuals, and a backslider who had been converted to Jesus at a Billy Graham Crusade, only to lose his new faith within the month. I remember him best. His name was Lawrence, and he weighed two hundred fifty pounds. I found him sitting on a dark stone wall surrounding an open air theatre, just off the beach. The wall was known as Hooker's Row, and all the youngest prostitutes in that part of town passed by it at least twice an evening. Lawrence wanted the Lord to make him thin, and we prayed for it together. I remember when he prayed he bowed his head so low his chin quadrupled. Sweat popped out on his forehead and rolled down his fleshy nose. He whispered "Amen," at the end of the prayer, and then looked at me anxiously. "Do you think he'll do it?"

I took a deep breath, listening to the far-off pounding waves. "You can't let your faith depend on whether God makes you thin or not. Maybe he has you fat for a reason."

This was at night, and I couldn't see his face unless he looked directly at me. I couldn't see what he was thinking. But his voice was still shaky from the prayer. "The reason I stopped believing before was because God didn't do anything when I asked him not to make me live alone forever. But women don't care if I have Jesus, they look at me the same now as they used to, because I'm still so fat. I think he could help me if he wanted to, but he won't."

"You can't afford to let being fat stand in the way of your salvation."

"Why can't I worry about it? Other people don't have to look like this, why should I have to? If God doesn't care that I'm lonely then what good is he?" He became quiet for a moment. I couldn't think of anything to say, I only waited, uncomfortable. He said, in a confidential tone, "I came here to get a woman tonight. You knew that, didn't you? People only come here for that—I don't mean *you*, though, I wasn't accusing you of anything like that." His eyes seemed to be softening. "I try to be good like you, but I have all these ugly thoughts all the time. I think about women from the time I wake up till the time I get to sleep. I can't keep from thinking about them, not even when I read the Bible, like you suggested. I tried that a million times. It doesn't work. If he wants me to be good, why does he give me all these thoughts?"

"You have to fight them. That's what they're there for."

"No it isn't. You can't fight them. It's like trying to fight getting hungry, you starve. If you get thoughts like that long enough, you'll just go crazy if you don't do something about them."

"Nobody every said it would be easy. But it's worth it in the end."

"I'll only end up here again," Lawrence said. After that he was quiet for a while. I gave him a long speech about joining a church. A church, I said, was like a fireplace full of glowing embers, and he was one of those embers who removed himself from the rest, slowly losing his share of the fire. I was really pleased with that metaphor. But I didn't carry it far enough. I didn't tell him there's only so much fuel in the universe, so far as we know. Every fire, no matter how large, has to go out sooner or later. The last thing Lawrence said to me was, "If God loves me, he'll make me skinny so I won't have to come here any more."

I couldn't answer that. I left him alone.

MOTHER LOAD

In some ways I never had a better year than freshman year. I didn't have much fun, but I felt clean—it's hard to explain if you've never been Christian. I've lost some feeling I had then—though maybe it was just an illusion—the feeling that I was sheltered between two giant hands, that I was always protected and loved by someone. When I was a freshman I still needed all that. I still thought of myself as a boy. I lived in a dorm room on North Campus, with two upper classmen.

That was back when rooms were still tripled because of overcrowding. This room was on the corner of Lewis's second floor, and supposedly it was tripled because it was bigger than other rooms, though I never noticed any difference in size. My mother and brothers brought me here, and helped me move in. I remember we had a hard time finding the right dorm. My younger brother Allen had a map of campus and read off directions to Mama, who quietly turned left, right, left; I looked out the window, not saying much. Cars swarmed on every conceivable strip of asphalt, middle-aged couples parking and unpacking for their sons and daughters. I was a little afraid, catching glimpses of all those strange faces. Finally Allen said, "Here it is," and Mama nodded without saying a word.

Lewis is so old the bricks look like they have wrinkles, like all the pictures you see of college dorms. I tucked in my shirttail and looked up at the blank windows. Mama faced me, but wouldn't look at me. "You better get your key, hadn't you? We'll unload."

Inside were voices and laughter, fathers talking to daughters, mothers making beds. At the check-in table, in a dark room furnished with vinyl-covered couches and a television set, I wrote on a yellow card all the information someone is always asking you to write on cards around here. The RA gave me my key and promised to come to my room soon, to welcome me here. I nodded as if I understood what an RA was or why he should care whether I came to Chapel Hill or not; but through a window I could see Mama wrestling one of my suitcases out of the trunk. She pushed hair off her forehead, looking small and tired.

I hurried outside to help. Mama glanced at me, restlessly smiling. "It ought not to take more than two trips, there's so many of us."

"The stairs are nice and wide too," I said.

My brother Duck said, "Hey Danny, you can play tennis!" The parking lot faced a tennis court, which was crowded even today. Allen and Duck clung to the fence, pressing their faces against the links. Mama said, "You boys come on back now, and help us unload. We have to get home before dark."

Everybody took something, even Grove. I tried to get there ahead of everybody else, to see what it looked like. The first time I opened the door, I had this sinking feeling everything had gone wrong somehow. Two iron beds stood bunked along one wall, and a single bed faced them from the wall opposite. Mama came in a few minutes after Allen and Duck got there. I watched her pan the room. She slowly set down the suitcase. "It's not very big."

"I don't guess I'll have to be in here all that much," I said. "I can study at the library or something."

"You ought to take this bed." She took a box of my books from Duck and set them on the single bed. Ivy on the window threw shadows across her arms. Duck jumped on the bed and said, "Boy, this is hard as a rock!"

Mama ran her hands over the mattress. "I hope it won't give you kidney trouble."

"There's a *board* underneath it! Look Allen, there's a *board* underneath."

"Get off the floor, Duck," Mama said.

"But there's a board under Dan's mattress."

"Get up *now*. I'm not going to tell you again."

"Boy this is neat. It's just like a bed of nails."

We unloaded the rest of my boxes, and I closed the door to shut out the noise from the room across the hall. Mama sat on my bed. "You want me to help you get settled in?"

"I can do it."

"Let me at least make your bed for you—" she raised her hands suddenly, as if she hoped they might say something she couldn't. In the silence we looked at each other, conscious of what was being broken now. My brothers leaned against the walls, arms crossed, becoming suddenly quiet. Mama said, "You'll come home on weekends."

"Oh yeah. And I'll write letters. And I can call sometimes too."

"You won't be lonesome. There'll be lots of studying to keep you busy."

"I can write you every week."

"It's really not far to drive. Some of your friends will probably be coming home on the weekend." She nodded, and nodded again. But the void was still there: me on one side of the room, her on the other, a pane of glass between us. I could see her, but it was as if I couldn't really reach her now. She was receding. Again she pulled her hair back. I wondered if she would send the other boys ahead. But no. Glancing at me, afraid, she gathered Allen and Duck and Grove to her sides—a look in her eyes as if they were tearing her arms away—she hugged me, touching my hair. "You be careful now, and make good grades so I can be proud of you."

"I will."

"You write me. And don't study all the time. Have a little fun now and then. And if you don't get your financial aid on time, I'll try to send you some money."

"I'll be okay."

I kissed her soft, dry cheek, and walked them outside. Allen and Duck got into an argument about who was going to sit in the front seat. At the car door Mama said, "Don't stand here while we drive away. Just go back inside." She glanced at me. "We have a long drive ahead of us."

She slid behind the steering wheel and closed the door. For a moment I wished—just wished, knowing this feeling wasn't right, this tearing. But I nodded to Mama through the car window, and walked away. Upstairs I watched from my window as they headed out of the parking lot. Through the windshield I could see her sitting so erect, gripping the steering wheel, staring straight ahead.

I shelved my books. From the adjacent rooms and buildings flooded the noises of my new classmates, falling onto my head so heavy I could only slowly sit on the bed; I remember I was holding a Bible Mama had given me, its red ribbon marker trailing across my wrist.

CHERRY

When I came to school that day I had never been drunk in my life, and I managed to hold out against the forces of dissipation my whole freshman year. I never went to parties, or if I went, I conspicuously didn't drink, so people would ask me about my temperance and I could witness to them about Christ.

But in the fall of my sophomore year I moved to Ehringhaus, which I liked better than Lewis. By then, I had stopped going to Campus Crusade meetings, and attended church less and less regularly. That fall, I went to my first PJ party.

At first I pretended I was just there to watch the other people get drunk. But the PJ was just fifteen cents a glass, and I didn't know how it felt to get drunk. I shelled out my nickels and dimes, and drank five glasses straight; only God knows how many I drank the rest of the night. I ended up lying under a bulletin board in the hall. Someone bent over me. "Do you want to go to bed?" she asked.

"Where?"

She laughed one of those laughs drunk people make, a fish-giggle. "In *your* room, silly, where do you think?"

"Oh, I don't know. I was hoping you could suggest something."

"How about the roof?"

"You want me to freeze? Just leave me alone, I'm comfortable here."

I remember dancing for a while. My stomach felt like one of those containers you mix chemicals in, the PJ sloshing up and down, all gooed up in this pizza I'd eaten for dinner. This was my first be-a-dorm-worm night. I even wore sneakers without socks. The girls all thought I was charming. "Would you like to dance?" a fat girl asked.

"No, I don't think I could take it."

"Why, too drunk?"

"No, but you might step on my foot, and that would be the end of my college career."

I think she was insulted. She waddled off in a huff. It occured to me the next day that fat girls have feelings too. A lot of things occured to me the next day. My roommate bopped me on the head with a pillow bright and early. "Hi roomie!" he shouted. "How do you feel this morning? You felt good last night."

My head felt like an echo chamber. Ten thousand rooms spun around me in colliding orbits. I resolved to die immediately, without fuss. I would jump off the balcony.

I got up and put on my pants, not thinking it proper etiquette to kill myself in the nude. On the balcony, the fresh air made me want to live again. I remembered I had sat on the balcony the night before, about the time the last glass of PJ bombed my red corpuscles. I flew as high as any weather balloon then. Over me, the stars arced poetic-ally. I let my feet hang over the edge, trying to seem forlorn.

I began to wonder why I'd gotten drunk.

I could see that first drink in my hand. The PJ was pink, with oranges and lemons floating in it. One cherry sat on top of the crushed ice.

I asked myself, Do you want to eat that cherry? Is that what you should do first?

The cherry was soft. I squeezed the juice out of it, red along my palms. I decided if I ate it, I had to do it good and nasty, so I pinched the cherry together till the meat burst out. The alcohol tasted sharp and bitter, my whole tongue contracting against it. I bit the cherry in half and chewed it slowly. By the end of that first bite I was already depraved. I drank with lust after that. I didn't drink to forget; I drank not to think at all. I wanted the alcohol to be like a bomb exploding inside my brain.

Why did I eat that cherry? I looked out the window. I didn't know anybody in that room, I didn't like parties; why did I begin anything so crazy?

I keep going around in circles. My mother had written me a letter that ended this way. *You have always been a good boy. You always listened to what I told you, and you never did the wild things your friends did. You never gave me the problems other teenagers gave their fathers and mothers. But now you're alone, and I worry about you. It's hard being so far away, I don't know what you're doing any more. I know people are doing wild things around you all the time, and I'm afraid you may start too. You know I mean drinking. Please remember you don't have to drink to have good times. People hardly ever drink for the right reasons.*

I felt as if she were at the party, watching me from behind, and I kept turning around to find her. Somehow she'd be able to tell I had started drinking. She'd look at my eyes and know by the color. I had a horror of hurting my mother. Whether it was wrong to drink or not didn't matter, it *was* wrong to hurt somebody, wasn't it? I drank the red stuff faster, to get it behind me. I went to use the bathroom. The lights glared fierce and cool, the bulbs giving off a low buzz, so that I felt surrounded by electrical energy. The bathrooms in Enringhaus are small boxes of green and white tile. Every movement you make echoes. I made enough noise for a dozen of me. The mirror told me I was just as ugly drunk as I was sober; I smiled at my own beauty. My teeth were pink. For some reason I decided to brush my teeth, and did. The brush came out with bits of cherry on the bristles.

I danced eight or nine dances after midnight, and somewhere in that part of the night is when I laid down under the bulletin board. Then somebody pulled me into the elevator and tried to take off my clothes, but I couldn't stand up long enough. I went to my room. I sat on the balcony, and stared at the lights over campus. I got sick, and threw up on the balcony. I went back to my room, and got into bed. As I slept, my head swelled to twice its size, and the water boiled out of my mouth. In the morning my tongue was a cinder and my head a living bruise. I spent the morning pretending I was a corpse, until my roommate got me up.

That was my first party.

GLASS

I would also like to tell you about the time I gave head to an icicle, during November of my sophomore year, after I'd locked my Bible in the trunk for good. My friend Anne and I were walking through campus one cold morning, when ice had settled over tree branches and grass like a sheet of glass. We cut through McCorkle Place, passing the frost-covered soldier and the gray obelisk, skating across the Old Well, sliding into the frosty bushes around it. Anne's face shone like a beacon in the cold.

I was first to reach South Building, running behind the

shrubbery to the yellow brick walls, hung with frozen ivy. I touched the dead ivy fibers, cleaning off frost, when underneath a brick window ledge I saw a single shard of ice, shaped like a spear head, so sharp I could have thrust it into my heart then and there with ease. This icicle I broke and held up for Anne, who graciously declined. I lifted it overhead, I only licked the tip a little, but my lips froze to it. I could only breathe till the melting ice freed me from touch, water dripping down my numb fingers. I let the icicle shatter on the brick sidewalk and wiped dry my hands. Anne said "That could have taken the skin off your mouth."

"It didn't, did it?"

"No, but it's still not an intelligent thing to do."

"Don't you like the cold? All us gray babies like cold weather." I broke an ice-covered branch off an oak older than anybody I know, as Anne cocked her head, her curious round eyes suddenly still. She said, "I only know why I like the cold, not why you do."

I smiled, dancing back from her, certain of my footing as if I were lighter than air. "It's not the cold, it's winter. I like the bleakness, the way trees are stripped to their outlines. Look how the ice covers them this morning. I feel more alone here in winter. Even in Chapel Hill you can hide things when it's cold."

Anne glanced at me, her face oblong and pale, her black collar turned up close to her face. "It's a dead time. How can *you* like deadness, you're the optimist."

"Winter is more alive than summer."

She nodded, but asked, "How?"

Between us stood two bare dogwood trees and one evergreen, full and thriving. I blew frost off bare dogwood branches and broke a prickly sprig of evergreen, brushing it across my palms. "The dogwood is dead now. All its pretty leaves and flowers are blowing around, drying up, gumming the bottoms of your shoes in the rain. But this—" I lifted the evergreen—"this is always alive, because it knows how to take the cold."

A cold wind came up, raising a chorus from the trees over Mc-Corkle Place, ripping through my hair like icy knives; leaves clattered at our feet, bitter voices; all this as the clouds overhead dropped down their load of softening light, the campus near day, cold and glittering, all glass. "What are you trying to say?"

"If you try to say it, it comes out sounding silly. But this dogwood is half-dead even when it's alive. It tries to hide from the cold, but cold is half the world. The evergreen never dies because it never forgets the cold."

"It's dead."

"It's beautiful. The cold is beautiful, walking on the edge of it is beautiful."

"I never said it wasn't." But she put her hands in her pockets and turned away a little. "I can believe it too. In Chapel Hill it's so easy to have faith in dead things. But you can end up crazy, falling in love with winter. Be careful Danny. The only reason to like the cold is because it makes you appreciate being warm at last."

She walked ahead of me down a tunnel of ice branches. I was supposed to follow, knowing she wanted me to. But I waited, watching as the patterns of winter-white light stroked her soft hair, the ice above her head like something you feel sometimes—cold like a hand gripping your stomach—when you look at a tree twisting upward into the sky like the arms of an old woman raised all knotted with veins and folds of old skin; I followed Anne slowly, but around me rose those women with their arms raised, covered with white ice that only made purer the note of the mourning song they sang as the cold wind stroked them to sleep again, rushing through their hair, stinging my face as it struck their twisted feet. Ahead on the path Anne slipped farther and farther beyond me, and I knew it was time to catch her. As if to agree with me, the wind rose and fell, the clouds closing together so tight the streetlights flickered on, filling hollow globes with light, forcing the emptiness back among the branches of ice. I laughed quietly. *Are you still there then? Turn on the lights just once. All of them.*

I laughed at myself a little, pushing forward through the solid cold, the air drawing stinging tears from my eyes; and for a moment I could see myself all made of glass: light or dark, I couldn't control what entered or did not enter.

DOUBTING THOMAS

Did you fill up my pipe yet? The matches are underneath that magazine. Don't worry, it's just *Newsweek*. I keep my dirty magazines hidden in a place where even the Lord couldn't find them. I'm drunk enough that I wouldn't mind showing you where they are, but they'd probably gross you out. It's amazing what you can buy pictures of. People will do anything for money. Right down on Franklin Street you can buy bottles of perfume that smell like sweaty crotches, or brassieres you can eat right off a girl's breasts. Really eat it, swallow it, digest it and everything.

Thomas is the one who got me started smoking dope though. We started smoking together when Thomas lived in Yum Yum

Apartments. He had this really ratty stereo back then, and he used to say he couldn't stand to listen to it unless he was too high to mind the pops in the speakers. I used to ask Thomas, "Do you know anybody who smokes more dope than you do?" and he'd always answer, "No, but I'd sure like to, if she was a girl."

The real answer to the question is yes, of course, there's people who smoke more than Thomas all over this town; there's people here who haven't been off marijuana since the Cuban missile crisis. Who can blame them, we all need a sedative now and then? Dope is like a slow bolt of lightning that soaks gradually through your entire body. It brings to life parts of your brain you never even used before.

Of course it's bad for you. Everything's bad for you. But in twenty minutes we could all be dead from a nuclear attack, so who cares anyway? Thera doesn't believe this, of course. I told you she argues with Thomas about drinking and smoking. One night, after one of these fights, Thomas got especially depressed. I found him in his room sitting by the edge of the bed, turning this album cover around and around in his hands. The bhong was in front of him, empty. I asked, "Would you like me to fill up the bowl?"

He gave me an odd look, as if he would have preferred that I simply fill the bowl and pass it to him without question. He picked up the bhong and tilted it from side to side. I could hear the ice-water rattling in the chamber. "You still high?" he asked.

"I'm doing okay. But I can stand another bowl if you can."

He gave me the odd look again, and set the bhong down. "Maybe we ought not to smoke any more."

I touched the rim of the bowl. "Is something wrong?"

"We smoke a lot of dope around here. Maybe we do it too much."

"Thera really got to you this afternoon, didn't she?"

He jammed his finger deep into the carpet pile. "I don't give a damn about that." He stared at the stereo receiver, soft green light falling from it to his hands. "It's just that I wonder why we smoke so much, sometimes. I wonder why I never get tired of it. Whenever somebody asks me if I want to smoke some, I want to say yes, whether I do it or not. It can't be right to want to do it so much, can it?"

I picked up the bhong myself, and filled the bowl while he watched. Even when I struck the match, he didn't say a word. I lit the bowl. Thomas had taught me to take really deep tokes, the kind you would imagine Linda Lovelace taking, where you suck the smoke straight down to the bottom of your lungs and let it canker for a while, holding it till you want to breathe so bad your eyes water. The blood beats right into the chambers of your ears, your head feels like pure solid light. I handed Thomas the pipe. He looked at it for a long time, but didn't look at me. Then he leaned slowly over the bhong and drew. It seemed like hours before he was finished. He leaned his head way back, his throat curved like a bow, tendrils of smoke rising from his pursed lips. We finished the bowl without a word. The music washed and hung and hovered and dropped like a live animal. Finally Thomas said, coolly, "Thank you sir." He shook his head. "But I don't think I want to smoke any more tonight."

He folded his hands together and studied them, quiet and almost motionless, swaying a little to the drum beat. I leaned against

Thomas's closet door. He glanced at me and said quietly, "I haven't said I'm going to give it up forever."

I only shook my head. There were candles in the room, one of them close to me, I think, wavering with my breath. Thomas asked, "What's wrong?"

"I don't know."

"Are you mad?"

I shook my head. I picked up the book of matches and dropped more leaves into the bowl, smoking it alone. I had reached the point where I usually retreated to my room, as if Thomas were silently asking me to leave, his door already closing in my face. He said, "If you're pissed off you could at least admit it."

"I'm not pissed off, I'm just tired."

"You're always tired."

"People make me that way."

He threw up his hands, wanting to say something about the way I hide from people; but I wouldn't let him. "Be quiet a while," I said. I listened a little longer to the music. The last song on the album began then, Bruce Springsteen's "New York City Serenade." I didn't get to hear it. Thomas said, "If you want to talk, that's fine, but if you're just going to sit there and pout, I wish you'd do it in your own room."

As far as I was concerned, that decided things. I closed the book of matches and rolled up my little baggy of dope. But as I stood, it occured to me I was being cowardly. Thomas didn't want me to leave, he wanted me to justify staying. I looked at him. "Do you know what you're doing?"

"Probably."

"She doesn't feel things the way you do, Thomas. She's scared to let herself go."

"That has nothing to do with smoking."

"Oh yes it does. She's afraid of dope most of all, because of all the things her parents have told her about it. It gives you something she can't, makes you feel something she can't make you feel. That scares her."

He touched the bhong gently. "I'd rather not talk about Thera this way," he said. "She can't help it." Then he sighed. "Sometimes I don't like Chapel Hill very much. You know?"

"Why?"

"It's like living in a town wrapped in cotton. Everybody here is so protected."

"It's a college town. College towns are like that."

He snorted. "Yeah. Full of adolescent little boys and girls so fresh off their mothers' laps they're afraid to go to the bathroom by themselves."

"The toilets are full of perverts."

"Behind every goddamn commode." He shook his head in disgust. "When they get away from school they won't have Mama and Daddy any more to tell them what's right and wrong. Then maybe they'll grow up."

I shook my head. "They won't have to, really. They'll just skate along doing what they're told. There's always somebody to tell you what to do."

"Why can't they leave me alone? I don't care what *they* do, as long as they don't always try to run me."

"There isn't any *they*. There's just billions of nerds who exist one at a time. They'll do to you whatever you let them do. But they're not that hard to avoid."

"We've missed the best part of the song," he said, and cued the album back to where it began. Then he looked at me and opened his hands. I could hear him telling me what to do. I opened my baggie and dropped a little powder into the bowl, and then lit it. The conversation was over. We had said everything we had to say on the subject. He smiled at me and took the bhong, letting it make love to his lungs. "I only wish I could teach her she doesn't have to grow up with her eyes closed," he said, and I nodded.

APPETITE CITY

You see, Joel, whether you live in Chapel Hill or Jamaica, the way things are set up in the cosmos you only get two choices. You can either forget about your doubts, or admit them. If you forget them, you're pretending that life is all rosy and ordered: you can sit content-edly in front of your television while it drones into your brain the single flat note of electricity that sustains you. You don't hurt, true, because you don't feel anything. The feelings you have only con-fuse you; it's best to avoid them entirely.

Or else you can say to yourself, I don't understand why all this hurts so much. I don't understand why I have to get up early every morning to go to a job I hate to earn money to live a life that's made empty by the fact that I have to go to a job I hate every morning; I don't understand why I stay married to a man who hates me in a house with children who shout at one another all day long; I don't understand why two martinis before dinner aren't enough anymore. At least you're feeling pain. When a person wants to learn how to be happy, he starts to examine every move he makes, till he's looking at everything so long and hard he can't help but feel them: even the smallest detail becomes so vital. There's so much joy locked away in the world, if we can only face the locks. A person can learn to use his appetites to keep himself human. Just as he can learn to use the thought of death to keep himself alive.

Now in all fairness to Thomas, about half that speech is his. What I just gave you are all the parts we left out of our conversation about smoking dope that night. Did you ever notice how, in conversations between friends, most of the really good parts are always left out, understood? I'm too far gone tonight to divide the different thoughts between us, so I took them all myself; since I'm the one telling this story, and since this *is* my closet.

In fact, I wanted to make up a party game about appetites, for tonight. Here's how you play. First you appoint a judge. (My mother would make a good one, but almost anybody's mother would do). Then you get everybody at the party together, and have them each think of the most depraved way imaginable for fulfilling one or another of the basic appetites. You can tell any kind of story you like, and you can put as many appetites into one story as you want to. The only real requirement is that you have to tell the whole story out loud, so everyone can hear it. It would be better if you told true stories. The winner of the game is the one whose story makes the judge the maddest.

The only catch to the game is that you can't really play it anywhere but in Chapel Hill, at least not in North Carolina. Chapel Hill understands that appetites are for learning. They're neither good nor bad. People who come to Chapel Hill with their appetites suppressed suddenly find them made welcome and at home. Chapel Hill doesn't have a value either. It simply exists, and you may come here or leave, as you choose. Some people actually get an education here, and become decent, respectable citizens of the ordered universe. Other people turn Chapel Hill into an enormous closet, in which to hide from the rest of the world. It's so easy to come here and never leave.

I like you, Joel. You have to come back to my closet again sometimes. But this pipe and this glass are both empty, and I'm ready to join the party again. I hope we won't both smell like dirty underwear; that would be embarassing, and hard to explain. Do you want to play the appetite game at this party? We can't get my mother to judge, but there's always Thera. I'd put my money on Thomas to take the crown, if she judges.

Or better yet, I think I might win it myself. I invented the game, didn't I? I'm as depraved as any Yankee ever was. When I open this door, you switch off the lamp. Maybe someday I really will fill up with light. That's the way angels look, I bet. There, my good sir, the closet door is open once again. Come to my party, won't you? I do hope you have a good time. My name is Danny Crell, and I am the King of Appetites. Welcome to Appetite City.